LUISA'S AMERICAN DREAM

by
Claudia Mills

FOUR WINDS PRESS   NEW YORK

*The characters and situations described in this book
are fictitious and are not to be mistaken
for real people or events.*

LIBRARY OF CONGRESS CATALOGING IN PUBLICATION DATA

Mills, Claudia.
  Luisa's American dream.

  SUMMARY: Cuban, Catholic, and poor,
14-year-old Luisa Ruiz wants the American dream
and finds it in the form of a young WASP with
money and sophistication. To win his love, she lies
about her background, and then discovers he's not
what she wants after all.
  [1. Cuban Americans—Fiction] I. Title.
PZ7.M63963Lu   [Fic]   80-69997
ISBN 0-590-07684-1

PUBLISHED BY FOUR WINDS PRESS

A DIVISION OF SCHOLASTIC INC., NEW YORK, N.Y.

PRINTED IN THE UNITED STATES OF AMERICA

LIBRARY OF CONGRESS CATALOG CARD NUMBER: 80-69997

1 2 3 4 5 85 84 83 82 81

To Beverly,
Barbara,
and Susan

CHAPTER

1

Luisa was sitting in a partially disassembled armchair with her mouth full of upholstery tacks, making a mental list of the things she hated. The list would have become unmanageable, but Luisa kept track of it in installments.

Number one, she thought, carefully removing the tacks from her mouth one by one, I hate upholstery and every single thing about it. Number two, nuns in general and Sister Bernice in particular. Number three, fattening black beans and rice, fattening bananas deep-fried in oil, and fattening guava pudding. . . . Well, not guava pudding. Her grandmother was bringing some over for supper, and maybe she would have just a little bit.

She tucked her feet up under her, sneezing as some ancient dust from the seat cushion's loose stuffing tickled her nose. She wished for the millionth time that she didn't have to work after school in her parents' reupholstery shop, instead of listening to records at her friends' houses—real houses they owned, with only their families living in them and no neighbors stomping around upstairs in the middle of the night. For that matter, she wished her parents didn't even have a reupholstery shop, taking up a perfectly good back bedroom. She looked with disgust at the untidy bolts of fabric and the wrecked chairs and sofas.

She wished she didn't go to a Catholic girls' school, and she wished Sister Bernice hadn't told her she had to do an extra algebra assignment for wearing lipstick. Our Lady of the Mountains must be the only school on the face of the earth, Luisa thought, where you couldn't wear makeup. If she lived today, even the Virgin Mary would wear at least lip gloss. Luisa giggled. She would have to tell that to Mary Beth and Karen.

"Luisa!" Mami called from the kitchen.

"Coming!" Luisa called back in Spanish. They still spoke Spanish at home, even though it had been ten whole years since they left Cuba for Bridgeport, Connecticut. Ten years since they took a "freedom flight" from Castro's Communist island to the United States, land of opportunity. At least, that's how Papi had described it. Luisa deposited the tacks in the open cabinet drawer and slammed it shut. Opportunity for someone else, maybe.

In the crowded little kitchen Mami stood by the stove, stirring the black beans that would be spooned over rice at dinner. How foresightful of Luisa to include them on today's hate list.

"I don't have enough bananas for supper. Could you run to the store for just a minute and get a bunch?" Mami asked.

"Fried bananas make you fat," Luisa said.

Luisa's mother was certainly fat—at five-foot-two she weighed a good hundred and seventy pounds. But she didn't seem hurt by Luisa's remark.

"José likes them so much," she coaxed, "and he works so hard at his soccer practice."

"I'll go," Luisa said. At least she'd get out of the re-upholstery shop for a while. "Joey'll have his bananas."

She decided that if she was going to run to the store she might as well really *run*. That way she could have a piece of guava pudding without feeling obese when she weighed herself in the morning. It wasn't easy staying halfway normal-sized in a house where no one ate anything besides sugar, starch, and fat. She crossed into the room she shared with her brother.

The room was divided by a draped sheet. Joey's half was spartan and bare. There were no decorations except for two sports trophies from Warren G. Harding High that Mami insisted on displaying, and, of course, the crucifix over the bed. Lucky Joey had gotten out of going to Catholic school; Papi thought four years in a public high school in Bridgeport would "make a man out of him." And from the look of Joey's side, Papi seemed to have achieved his goal. There were no posters on the splotchy walls and no photographs. Even the bed looked flat and hard, since Joey slept without a pillow.

But if Joey's half of the room reflected Papi's idea of masculinity, Luisa's was all feminine. There were posters, mostly of Robert Redford, all over the walls, and the bureau was cluttered with bottles of perfume, makeup, and heart-shaped enamel boxes overflowing with earrings and hair ribbons. She had seventeen stuffed animals, from the childhood rabbit that was all she had been allowed to bring from Cuba, to an enormous lime-green panda Joey's friend Tom had won for her at the boardwalk last summer. Luisa picked up the rabbit now and gave it a hug, examining the places where the fur was wearing thin. She still remembered holding it tightly in all the confusion at the airport, where long lines of people waited to leave Cuba, perhaps never to return.

It had been a few months after Castro initiated his policy of unrestricted emigration, following the long years when it had been virtually impossible to leave. Immediately after the revolution the wealthy and propertied, who had enjoyed their fortunes undisturbed under the Batista dictatorship, had fled by the tens of thousands to the capitalist land to the north. The Ruiz family had stayed behind, naturally.

The Ruizes hadn't been poor before the revolution, but they had hardly been rich. Papi had been a foreman in the sugar processing plant outside Cabañas, the coastal village where they lived, west of Havana in the Pinar del Río province. It was better than cutting cane in the fields—at least he wasn't unemployed during the off-harvesting season—but he worked as long and hard as any laborer.

They had thought everything would be better under Castro, the bold, bearded revolutionary who hid out in the Sierra Maestra, preaching his gospel of democracy, equality, and economic prosperity. Everybody had thought so. But things hadn't gotten any better. Well, they had for a lot of people, Luisa knew; certainly for the illiterate poor who, before Castro, had lived hungry in their rural shacks. But for the Ruizes there had been just the rationing, endless lines to buy an iron or an alarm clock, and the neighbors across the street, watching from behind closed blinds for any offenses they could report to the Committee for the Defense of the Revolution.

Papi and Mami had assumed it wouldn't last; Castro would be overthrown in turn. Lots of people, like Papi's brother Ramón, were plotting a counterrevolution, to be coordinated with an American-backed invasion by Cuban exiles in the Bay of Pigs. But the plot failed. Alerted in time, Castro made massive arrests of suspected dissenters. Expected American support for the invading force never materialized, and the exile invaders were left to fight alone, to a brief and ignominious defeat. Ramón had gone to prison for three years, and even Papi had been questioned over and over again.

The year after, reports leaked into the United States that the Soviet Union was secretly building long-range missile sites in Cuba. After the tense confrontation following this discovery, all commercial air service between Cuba and the United States had been discontinued. Then, in 1965, Castro announced that everyone was now free to leave; anyone who didn't want to stay and work for the revolution wasn't welcome in Cuba, anyway.

The Ruizes had left as soon as they could. They had been flown by the United States government to Miami, where Luisa's uncle Miguel had lived since the fifties. From there, they had taken a bus north to Bridgeport, joining Mami's parents and her younger sister, Consuela. Since Consuela and her husband had emigrated several years before the rest of the family, they helped Papi find a home and a job on the assembly line at American Consolidated Can. And there the Ruizes were still. Bridgeport, the "Park City." The "Parking Lot City" would be more like it. Luisa gave the rabbit another gentle squeeze and put him back on the big panda's lap.

If she stood all day looking at her stuffed animals, she'd never get to the store for Joey's bananas. She quickly laced up her running shoes—just Woolworth's, but they looked like Adidas—clipped back her waist-long dark hair, and flew down the stairs to the street.

She ran along East Main Street at a good pace. Some of the men lounging in the bar doorways shouted at her, but she didn't look in their direction. Living in Bridgeport on the East Side for so long, she had learned to ignore the whistles of drunkards. There were six bars to pass on her way to the little Spanish grocery where her mother bought yucca and guava paste and green bananas, and even though it was just afternoon, all were full.

Luisa was glad Papi and Joey didn't drink—at least not

much. Well, Joey did drink more than Mami and Papi would like. He smoked marijuana, too. He had a little plastic bag of grass and a pipe hidden in one of his bureau drawers. She would have found them when she put away his clean underwear and socks, but he had told her about them, anyway. Joey and Luisa knew they could trust each other with any secret.

She was panting from the run by the time she reached her destination. Luisa really liked the Spanish grocery store and the tempting bakery next door, in spite of herself. Their owner, Mr. Alfonso, knew her grandfather, *Abuelo,* and he always teased Luisa about "all her sweethearts"—there weren't any—and asked how much Abuelo had won in the numbers. Abuelo played the numbers every day, like almost every man Luisa knew, except Papi. Everyone had gambled back in Cuba, too, until Castro did away with gambling. Usually Abuelo lost, of course, but once he had won five hundred dollars, and he and *Abuela,* her grandmother, had taken a trip to Miami and Key West to visit relatives.

After picking out an enormous bunch of heavy green bananas, Luisa took the big, unwieldy bundle and jogged off toward home. The sun was sinking lower in the sky. In a couple of weeks, when they all set their clocks back, it would be dark at this time. She quickened her pace and darted across East Main Street.

Suddenly, there was a screech of brakes. The blue Mustang that had been speeding down the street skidded to a halt, barely missing her. Startled, Luisa tripped over the curb and fell hard on the pavement, the bag of bananas flying out of her arms.

She lay still for a minute, feeling dazed. She heard footsteps and then a male voice shouting at her angrily,

"Why the hell don't you look before you run out in the street like that?"

To her surprise, Luisa started to cry. She didn't cry much, and the fall hadn't really hurt her, just scraped her knees, but it had knocked all the cool out of her. She lay on the sidewalk, tears trickling down her cheeks.

"Hey." The guy reached out and helped her to sit up, holding his arm around her to steady her. "Are you all right?"

Luisa turned to look at him for the first time, and she could hardly believe what she saw. He seemed about her brother's age, maybe a little bit older, and certainly more handsome than all her poster idols put together, with blond, curly hair, deep-blue eyes, and a strong, confident chin. She was also aware of the solid muscularity of his arm, resting against her shoulders.

She managed a shaky smile. "Sure. I'm okay."

"Listen, can I drive you home?" he asked, gesturing toward the blue Mustang. "Since you just managed to leave my car in one piece."

"No, thanks," Luisa said, standing up slowly. "I'd better finish running. It's my new school year's resolution."

"I have another resolution for you," he said, and she waited, holding her breath.

"Look both ways before you cross the street."

He smiled, and she laughed. "I'll write it down when I get home."

He headed for his car, and Luisa started running, faster than she usually did and more gracefully, so that he would be impressed—not that guys were romantically intrigued by girls' athletic achievements. But once the car had rounded the corner she stopped, suddenly aware of her smarting knees and Joey's bananas, left somewhere on the pavement where she'd fallen. She hadn't really forgotten them. She just hadn't wanted him to see her picking up a gigantic bunch of swollen Spanish bananas.

She limped back to retrieve them. They were still there. The bag was torn, but only one banana was noticeably bruised, and it was not bruised, Luisa thought, as badly as her knees. She decided to break the running resolution, which she had just invented, anyway, so she could have an excuse to decline his offer of a ride, and walked home slowly.

She knew the guy with the blue Mustang wasn't from the East Side. He didn't seem to be from Bridgeport at all. He probably knew that she was, though, since runners hardly congregated from around the world to jog down East Main Street. But at least she hadn't let him give her a ride home! Then he would have known for sure that she lived on Tilden Street, just three doors down from the Good Times bar.

When she reached home she looked at it with newly critical eyes—though she had been plenty critical before—trying to see it as he would have. The shabby two-story house, where the Ruiz family rented the ground floor and the Martinezes the upstairs, needed painting badly. The low chain-link fence around the little pocket handkerchief of lawn was broken in places. She counted three beer bottles on the dying grass. At least, she thought bitterly, there was no sleeping drunk blocking the driveway, where the secondhand van her father used in furniture deliveries was parked, as there had been one morning last week. Her parents had called the police, and they had come and carted him away.

She picked up the bottles and threw them, hard, into the garbage cans, which stood between the house and the street. He would never drive down Tilden Street, she knew, and if he did, he wouldn't know it was her street. Still, the place didn't *have* to look like a pigsty.

"Luisa! You've been so long, I've been worried. Oh, baby, what happened to your knees?" Mami babbled on in her rapid-fire Spanish.

"I fell running," Luisa snapped, and laid the bananas on the table.

"Let me put some iodine on them and bandage them for you," Mami said.

"They'll be all right." But Mami made her sit down, anyway, and, taking Luisa's legs one after the other across her ample lap, she washed out the cuts, applied some stinging iodine, and deftly bandaged them, all the while talking.

"The Bernsteins want three more couches reupholstered," she said, "and they said that several of their friends had seen what we did with the loveseat and are going to call us soon with orders." Who cares? Luisa thought, setting her teeth for the iodine. "So we will have our hands full with the business this fall, all of us. Maybe soon your father can leave his job at the factory and work with me in the shop full-time. Oh, and did you see, we had these cards printed up." She showed one to Luisa as she gave a last, loving pat to the neat bandage. "Ruiz Reupholstering. Good service. Low prices," she read in English, and laughed proudly.

"They're nice," Luisa commented mechanically, and impatiently swung her legs down. "I better go get changed," she said. She wanted to be alone, just for a few minutes, if that wasn't too much to ask. She went into her room, hoping Joey wouldn't be there. She heard the sound of the shower. That was good. Joey's showers took at least two hours.

She lay facedown on the bed, not caring if her dirty

sneakers soiled the bright-flowered bedspread Mami had made her from some leftover drapery material. She hated living in Bridgeport. She hated living in a house where laundry hung shamelessly across the back porch. And she hated being Cuban. She had met the most absolutely beautiful guy in the universe, and she would never see him again.

"Luisa! José! Abuela and Abuelo are here! It's time for dinner!"

Luisa pulled off her T-shirt and folded it reverently. Maybe she would never wash it. But, she giggled suddenly, it did smell to high heaven. She wadded it into a ball, kissed it, and stuffed it into the laundry bag. She would see him again, she promised herself. She just had to.

CHAPTER

2   "Have some more rice and black beans," Luisa's mother urged her at dinner.

"I'm full," Luisa said.

"How about some more pork, just a little bit?"

"I said I was full." She wasn't going to look like a balloon the next time she saw the guy in the blue Mustang.

"Aw, lay off her, Mami," Joey pitched in. "You just want everyone to be as fat as you are." He shot his mother one of those sudden grins that took any sting out of his teasing.

"How is she going to grow if she doesn't eat?" Abuela asked.

"I've grown all I'm going to grow," Luisa said.

"All grown up," Mami said fondly, stroking Luisa's cheek. "Oh, that reminds me, this family has some very important plans to make." She winked across the table at Papi.

Luisa knew that Mami was referring to her *quince*. In Cuba girls had a "sweet fifteen" rather than a "sweet sixteen" party, and every family prided itself on giving its daughters the most elaborate *quince* it could afford. Many rented out a hall and hired a band, and all invited relatives from far and wide.

Luisa was going to be fifteen in December, and if there was one thing she didn't want for her fifteenth birthday, it was a *quince*. It was bad enough to *be* Cuban; she didn't have to advertise it with a huge, crowded, noisy Cuban celebration. The only good thing about the *quince* was that her parents would let her start dating afterward. It was supposed to be her "coming out" party, her debut as a young lady in society. Some society, though.

11

"It's still a long way off," she said, hoping that they would forget about it until it was too late for any grand plans.

"A long way!" Abuela moaned, wringing her hands. "We should have been making plans for months already. But your mother is always so late, she won't listen to me—"

"It's okay, Abuela," Joey said. "There's still plenty of time."

"We don't have to make it all that big a deal, anyway," Luisa suggested.

"Not a big deal?" Papi asked, pushing himself slowly back from the table. Papi was almost as fat as Mami. "The *quince* of my pretty girl?"

"Hey, it's time for the game," Joey said, catching his sister's eye. She returned his look gratefully. It was the second night of the World Series, and the Cincinnati Reds had beaten the Yankees in the first game, 5 to 1. Papi and Abuelo had both been Yankee fans their whole lives, even back in Cuba. They would come home from the sugar refinery in the evenings and listen to *beisbol* on the radio.

"Hey, José," Papi said, once he had put his feet up and made himself comfortable in front of the TV, "you tell your friend Tom to get out his handkerchief. He's going to need it to cry on."

"He said to tell you that if all the Cincinnati players showed up wearing blindfolds and had both arms tied behind their backs, the Yanks might stand a chance."

"We'll see, we'll see," Papi chuckled.

Tom Sachetti had been Joey's best friend from the day they met on the blacktop behind the Saint Charles School, right after the Ruiz family moved to Bridgeport.

Joey hadn't known any English, and some kids had been taunting him—Spanish kids, too, some of whom hadn't spoken such fluent English themselves in the not so distant past. Joey had borne with their teasing, until a couple of boys began throwing handfuls of gravel at him. He fought then, and Tom joined him. They came home together with three black eyes between them, permanent friends. They were both seniors at Harding High now, and they even talked of going to college together.

Tom spent more time at the Ruizes' house than he did at his own, three blocks away. His parents had been killed in a hit-and-run car accident before he was old enough to have any memories of them, and he had been brought up by his aunt Liz. Because she worked the evening shift at the Discount City supermarket, Tom spent most of his free evenings studying with Joey or watching the ball game with Papi, rooting against the Yankees with the same steadfast determination with which Papi rooted for them.

Luisa hated baseball, absolutely hated it. It wasn't so much the game itself, but seeing her father and grandfather in their undershirts, with their beer bellies hanging over their belts, sitting in front of the huge color TV with the cable receiver on top, shouting about a stupid ball game. And those smelly cigars that Abuelo was always smoking. He stank up the whole house whenever he came over. She made a mental note to add cigars to her hate list.

The three women cleared the table. Luisa washed the dishes, while Abuela covered up the leftovers—not a very big job, Luisa thought, in a family of human hogs. Mami made some strong, sweet Spanish coffee to serve the men in little demitasse.

Luisa actually didn't mind doing dishes. It was satisfying to swish the dirty plates and glasses through sudsy water and have them emerge sparkling. She didn't even mind that while she was doing the dishes, Joey sat watching TV. She had for the most part gotten over thinking that was unfair, because she was so used to it. Besides, Joey did so many things for her—like stealing her bike back from the kids down the street, who had stolen it from her. She had been furious when her bike disappeared from the rack in front of the public library. But Joey had just waited until he saw it leaning against a parking meter outside of Lou's Variety Store and had ridden it home.

Then she saw little Abuela, with knee-high stockings rolled down around her swollen ankles, scrubbing away at the top of the stove where some grease from the fried bananas had splattered, and she felt a spasm of dislike for her grandfather, who sat ensconced in the padded reclining chair that matched her father's. He didn't work anymore; he just sat at home all day in front of the TV, chewing on those repulsive cigars. He could really do more to help Abuela—even if it wasn't the way of Cuban men.

"I'll finish that, Abuela," Luisa volunteered.

"No, see, it's all done." Abuela stepped back to admire her work.

"Would you like a little more pudding?" Abuela asked. "I made it special for you."

Luisa surrendered. "Yes," she said, "your puddings are just too delicious." She patted her stomach regretfully, and cut off another slice of the firm, smooth bread pudding filled with little pockets of guava jelly. She ate slowly, savoring every bite.

"What happened to your knees?" Abuela asked.

"She fell when she was running to the store," Mami explained. "One of these days you and José are going to get run over, running everywhere the way you do. That's America, everyone in a big hurry. In my country people take things slow, easy. There's always tomorrow."

"Not anymore," Abuela said. "Not since the revolution. Now there are five-year plans just like in Russia, and everybody has to work for a ten-million-ton sugar harvest. Do you remember, one year your uncle Carlos wrote us that Castro said there was to be no Christmas, not until all the sugar cane was in? But was there any ten-million-ton harvest? Just more shortages and more lines. You never knew Cuba, baby," she said to Luisa. "It all ended before you were born."

"Not all the changes were bad," Luisa said. She hated it when Mami and Abuela went on and on about the good old days before the revolution.

"Don't let your father hear you say things like that," Mami warned. "As far as he is concerned, Castro made everything one hundred percent worse."

"But he didn't," Luisa said, not that she knew or cared anything about it. All she knew was that she was tired of hearing everyone rave about the past.

"There is more equality now," Mami conceded. "And I think they are telling the truth when they say that no one is hungry anymore. And in Cuba, even with the socialized medicine, the doctors still make house calls. Not here, no way! But it was so different, baby. So many people afraid, and just working, working all the time, and then having to volunteer to work more on the weekends."

"And they said you couldn't be a good communist if you went to mass!" Abuela stopped to cross herself.

"And everyone was so gay and happy before," Mami said. "All right, not everyone," she added, as she saw Luisa ready to object, "but we were carefree, my sister and I. And now the women work all day, side by side with the men, and leave their children with strangers— little children, babies even. It isn't right."

Luisa wondered how carefree Mami's life in the United States was, working all day in the reupholstery shop. But Abuela's question about her skinned knees had reminded her that it was time for her nightly phone call to Mary Beth. She just had to talk to someone about the guy in the blue Mustang, and there was no one else she could tell.

Mary Beth was also in the sophomore class at Our Lady of the Mountains, but the girls lived too far apart—on opposite sides of Bridgeport—to see each other on school nights. They spent part of almost every weekend together, however, usually at Mary Beth's house.

The Murphys didn't have much money, either, and, with Mary Beth's four sisters and three brothers, their house seemed small. Still, Luisa liked going there better than bringing Mary Beth home. Even if their big, old, white house was crowded, it was crowded with Murphys and not with Martinezes, and they had a long, rambling front porch with a swing to sit on in the summertime, and a real backyard with green grass. And Mrs. Murphy seemed more like a real mother—she wasn't always singing silly Spanish songs and dancing heavy, clumsy rumbas, the way Mami did.

Mary Beth was Luisa's closest friend and confidante. Only to Mary Beth—and to Tom—did Luisa confide her shame about being Spanish and poor. She couldn't tell her brother, since she knew that while he wasn't exactly thrilled about residing on the elegant Avenue de Tilden, as he called it, he was proud of Papi and Mami and what they had achieved, starting out from scratch in a new country. He had told Luisa once, when she was complaining about Mami's broken English, that it was pretty low to be ashamed of your family and your heritage.

Karen Cuffner, Luisa's second-best friend, tried to be understanding, but she thought it would be great to be Spanish or Italian or Polish—to have some ethnic identity. Karen was white, Anglo-Saxon, and Protestant. She went to Our Lady of the Mountains just because her parents had some crazy idea that it was academically superior to secular schools. Karen complained about being a WASP because it was such a big fat nothing. But Luisa would trade with her any day of the week. The guy in the blue Mustang was about as WASP as they came.

"I have to make a phone call," Luisa explained to Mami and Abuela, as she disappeared into the bathroom with the telephone receiver, locking the door behind her. The cord didn't reach into her bedroom, and she wasn't about to talk to her friends with Mami and Abuela, the two nosiest people in the whole world, listening to every word. Even if they didn't understand spoken English very well, there wasn't much that either of them missed.

"*¿Qué pasa?*" Mary Beth asked when she answered the phone. She was taking first-year Spanish at school. Luisa did most of Mary Beth's homework for her, which explained why Mary Beth did so well on the homework and so poorly on the quizzes, to the Spanish teacher's bewilderment.

"I'm in love," Luisa whispered.

"I can't hear you," Mary Beth said. "My stupid brothers are yelling about some touchdown in the World Series."

"Home run," Luisa corrected. She could hear Papi's groan of disappointment and disgust. Cincinnati must have scored. She raised her voice. "I said, I'm in love."

"Oh, that's right, I forgot. *Butch Cassidy and the Sundance Kid* was the four-thirty movie today."

"No, not Robert Redford."

"That guy we saw two weeks ago at the Laundromat, the one who looked like a lifeguard?"

"Someone new. He almost ran over me in his car while I was running." Luisa told Mary Beth the whole story.

"You were crazy not to let him drive you home. Who knows, maybe you two would have gone for a little ride, down to Seaside Park, and then it would have been too beautiful down there to stay in the car, so he'd have parked and opened the door for you, and then you would have walked along the beach, with his arm around your shoulders, you know, kind of protectively—"

"This is getting very silly," Luisa scolded, enormously pleased with Mary Beth's predictable reaction. But then she remembered just why she hadn't wanted him to drive her home.

"And then he'd have asked me where I live," she continued, "and I'd have directed him to Tilden Street. I'd have said, first you pass three bars and then turn left at Good Times. You can't miss it. It's the one with the beer cans all over the yard and the drunk passed out in the driveway."

"Listen," Mary Beth told her. "If he's the right kind of guy, he won't care where you live or how much money your parents have or whether they speak English. If he's not, then you might as well find out right away and save yourself a lot of time and trouble."

"I'll never see him again, anyway."

"Sure you will. We'll form a club to find him—we'll be the WASP-in-a-Blue-Mustang patrol. We haven't had any clubs for a long time, you know, and I think it's about time for a new one."

"Remember the Hate Sister Bernice club?"

"And Bra Wearers United?"

"And the Organization for Stamping Out Boys?"

"Well, there's not going to be any stamping out boys this time."

"What do we do first?" Luisa asked, with growing excitement. Even though she was too old now for secret signs and passwords and all that, the club did seem like a fun idea. And with old super-sleuth Mary Beth on his trail, the WBM didn't stand a chance.

"Well, we have two big clues. He's not from Bridgeport, and he drives a blue Mustang. Do you remember the license plate?"

"No, but I would've if it had been out of state."

"Any school jacket or blazer?"

Luisa marveled at her friend's detective instincts. "Yes! He was wearing a white sweater with a blue T on it."

"Trumbull," Mary Beth pronounced. "It fits perfectly. So this weekend, after you finish up in the shop, we'll make Joey drive us to the Trumbull shopping center, and then we'll take off on a thorough search of driveways. Phase One will be under way."

"I'd never have remembered the sweater if you hadn't asked that question," Luisa praised her.

"And I'll never remember that Spanish dialogue tomorrow if you don't help me practice. *¿Dónde queda la parada del autobús?*"

CHAPTER

3

After Mary Beth had recited the entire dialogue to Luisa's satisfaction, the WBM patrol members hung up, with plans to meet on Saturday at two. Luisa debated calling Karen to bring her up to date, and decided against it. Karen had a different attitude toward boys, probably because she already had guys calling her for dates, guys she had met at the Episcopalian church youth group in Weston, the exclusive suburb where she lived, or at the country club her parents belonged to. Karen had all the WASPs in blue Mustangs that she could handle. The news about Luisa's could wait until school tomorrow.

"Who's winning?" Luisa asked Papi and Abuelo, but she didn't need to, since their glum looks gave her all the information she needed.

"Cincinnati, three to zero," Joey said.

The phone rang. "I feel sorry for anyone trying to call a family with a fourteen-year-old daughter," Papi said. It was Tom, asking for Papi.

"Tell him I have better things to do," Papi said. "Ask him what he expects, with the Yankees' star pitcher and hitter both on the bench with strained muscles."

Joey called back from the phone, "He says he's coming over, and bringing that handkerchief you told him to get out. He says he can't believe you knew you'd be needing it."

"Just he wait!" Luisa's father shouted in English, loudly enough so that Joey didn't need to repeat it. Probably loudly enough for Tom to have heard without benefit of the telephone, Luisa thought.

Joey returned to the living room, grinning. He didn't

root for any team himself, so he got a big bang out of Papi and Tom's constant rivalry.

Luisa was glad Tom was coming over. With his dark, Italian coloring and muscular stockiness, people often thought Tom was a third Ruiz sibling. And Luisa sometimes wished that he were her brother instead of Joey. He seemed to understand more how she felt about things, how she could love Mami and Papi and yet wish they were different, more like other people's parents. At least he listened to her when she complained, without constantly picking on her the way Joey did.

She remembered one time when she and Mami and Joey and Tom had gone shopping downtown by the train station. There had been a big table in one store heaped high with sale merchandise, all in a great, confused jumble: men's T-shirts more or less at one end, and ladies' bras and panties at the other. How embarrassed Luisa had felt as Mami went digging through all the $1.99, size-forty bras, right in front of Tom and Joey and everyone. Joey had been laughing and teasing Mami, mimicking underwear commercials in a high falsetto voice. Tom had caught Luisa's eye and smiled—not an amused smile or even a sympathetic, pitying smile, but the smile of someone who understood.

The Yankees scored twice and everyone brightened up. Mami brought out a packaged, store-bought banana cream pie and passed out pieces. A pie didn't last very long with Mami cutting, that was for sure. Luisa didn't have any, but Mami, shooting an apologetic look in her direction, had seconds.

Tom walked in just as the Yankees scored again, tying the game 3 to 3. He was followed by Roberto, Papi's youngest brother, and his pretty wife, Anna. Roberto was smiling broadly and everyone knew what that meant: Roberto had won at jai alai.

"How much did you win?" Joey asked from across the room, in English, now that Tom was there.

"Enough," Roberto said, taking a satisfied swig from the opened beer bottle Mami had immediately placed in his hand.

Roberto was the best-educated and most American of Luisa's relatives. He spoke English fluently, with only a slight accent, and he was more successful in the new country than anyone except his brother Miguel, whose Cuban-American restaurant in Miami had made Miguel a wealthy man practically overnight. Roberto worked in New York City for an international import/export firm with an office in the World Trade Center. The company sent him on business trips to Bolivia and Peru, even to England and Scandinavia. He and Anna went to the movies often, and he prided himself each year on having seen all the Academy Award nominees and formed opinions on the outcome of the prize-giving. Roberto was definitely Luisa's favorite uncle.

"The games were especially exciting tonight, I think," Anna chattered on animatedly. There was something about her careful makeup and somewhat artificial gestures that reminded Luisa of a wind-up, talking doll. "Didn't I say that to you in the car, Roberto, that the players had been particularly good? It's almost like the ballet." Anna had never been to a ballet.

Everyone Luisa knew went to the jai alai fronton, or stadium, to watch the swift and graceful players, most of whom had come all the way from Spain, compete in a dazzling Basque version of handball. It was fascinating to watch the speed and ease with which they would dart to catch an almost invisible ball in the long, curved baskets that were fastened to their wrists, and then, in one sudden motion, hurl it against the wall.

But the real lure of jai alai was the opportunity it provided to gamble on the individual games. Jai alai gambling had been legal in Connecticut for several months, and those who tired of playing the daily numbers at Lou's Variety Store or found the odds of the state lottery too discouraging now went to jai alai instead. Papi usually went twice a week, sometimes taking Luisa and Joey along. He'd suddenly feel lucky, and without saying anything to anybody, would just take off in the van for the jai alai fronton. Papi would win twenty dollars or lose twenty dollars and then come home.

But Roberto was a master. He knew the players, he once boasted, as well as he knew Anna and Bobby, his five-year-old son. He studied their records and styles of play, and was able to predict with astonishing accuracy how they would fare in competition against one another. No one knew exactly how much Roberto had won at jai alai, but Luisa and Joey had often seen him win two or three hundred dollars in an evening. Joey figured that Roberto's winnings had passed the ten-thousand-dollar mark, and since he and Anna still lived on East Main Street, in half of the two-family house Anna's widowed father Jaime owned, Joey said he must be putting away a very nice bundle for Bobby's education, or to buy a big house outside Bridgeport.

"How's Sister Bernice?" Tom asked, settling down beside Luisa with his thick wedge of pie. "Want a bite?" He offered her his fork.

She shook her head. "More hateful than ever. She's launched a new anti-makeup campaign, her chief weapon being extra algebra assignments."

"I think Sister Bernice is right," Tom said, eyeing Luisa critically.

"Then you are no longer my friend," she rejoined.

"No, wait a minute. I don't think she's right to forbid you to wear makeup or to make you factor extra quadratic equations if you do. Though, as I remember from a certain math quiz I helped you study for, additional practice in algebra might not be such a bad idea."

"You just reminded me," Luisa said, "that one of those marvelous, helpful extra problem sets awaits me in my room."

"Aw, stay awhile longer," he said. "I just meant that I think girls look better without makeup."

"That's because some girls don't know how to use it right and walk around with bright-green eyelids."

"No, I like *you* better without it. You don't have it on now, right?"

"Yes, so what?"

"And you did have it on yesterday."

"Someone's pretty observant."

"Well, I think you look better tonight."

"Is that supposed to be a compliment about tonight or an insult about yesterday?"

"Just a fact." He smiled, and Luisa, in spite of herself, smiled, too.

"Like it's a fact that Cincinnati's going to win the series in four," he said, raising his voice for Papi's benefit.

Papi tittered scornfully.

The next player who came to bat was Cuban, and Papi emphatically motioned to everyone to be quiet, as if he didn't want Mami's loud laughter to disturb Hernando Cruz's concentration when Cruz faced the pitcher. The ball soared to center field for an easy double, and Papi beamed with satisfaction. "See," he said, *"Cubano."*

"Your father's really a proud Cuban," Tom remarked, smiling. "It makes me wonder how he could have left."

"Sometimes I think he and Mami left just because they couldn't get fat enough there."

Tom laughed.

"But, really, there were lots of reasons. Everything was rationed so strictly, and no matter how much money you had, you couldn't buy more than the official quota of meat, or coffee, or whatever, except on the black market, and you had to wait on long lines to get it. I remember Mami going around to some of the neighbors, trying to trade some old clothes for extra butter. She could have gotten into a lot of trouble if she'd been caught—and you could never tell who might turn you in for not having enough 'revolutionary spirit.' "

"There must have been other reasons, too, to make them leave everything."

"Well, Papi had wanted to leave ever since my uncle Ramón went to jail after the Bay of Pigs. You'd hear all the time about arrests and people going to prison, but when it was someone you knew, your own brother, you got scared. Besides, a lot of our relatives had already left. My uncle Miguel left back in the fifties, before the revolution, and he had this fancy restaurant in Miami. I guess Papi thought maybe he would start his own restaurant, too, or something, and make a lot of money."

"Did he ever try to start one?"

"Once—he and Roberto went into it together—but it didn't work out. So here we are in Bridgeport. Instead of working in a sugar factory, he works in a can factory. Big difference. Only Papi says at least you can say whatever you want here, and go wherever you want, and even if you fail at something, you still have a chance to try."

"And you can eat whatever you want," Tom added.

"And as much as you want," Luisa said. "But now, off to do algebra."

She got up reluctantly and kissed Mami and Papi and Abuelo and Abuela and Roberto and Anna. She and Joey didn't kiss all that much, but tonight she kissed him, too. And then, since he was the only one left, she bent over and gave Tom a soft kiss on the cheek.

"Hey, hey, hey!" he said, pretending to swoon.

Luisa tweaked his nose.

CHAPTER

4

Luisa and Mary Beth talked about the expedition to Trumbull for the rest of the week, passing notes back and forth right under Sister Bernice's beaked nose. They told Karen about it in the girls' room at lunchtime, and she just said, "You guys are crazy."

"We guys are geniuses," Mary Beth said.

"What if he keeps it in the garage? What if he's out driving it around? What if he doesn't live in Trumbull at all?"

"But what if he does?" Mary Beth replied. "Besides, this is just Phase One."

"What's Phase Two?"

"First let's see how Phase One turns out," Mary Beth said.

Karen finished retying the slender, green-velvet ribbon that held back her light-blond hair. Her reflection in the mirror over the sink looked troubled. "I know I sound like the pooper," she said, "but I have one more question."

"What is it?" Luisa asked. Everything seemed so simple and straightforward when she was talking to Mary Beth. Karen always made everything so complicated.

"What if you do find him, after all, and he turns out to be a real *jerk*? I mean, you've talked to him for about two minutes total—"

"You can tell a lot in two minutes," Luisa said. She remembered those blue eyes looking right into hers, and his arm around her, in the Trumbull letter sweater. If there was one thing the guy in the blue Mustang wasn't, it was a jerk.

"Well, good luck on Saturday," Karen said, sounding

27

as if she meant it. "And I bet you do find him, one way or another. I wouldn't put anything past you two."

On Saturday morning Luisa got up early, so early that she had to tiptoe through Joey's half of the room not to wake him. She started working right away in the shop. If she was going to finish in time to go to Trumbull, she'd have to hurry. But everything went even slower than usual—and not nearly as smoothly. She cut into one enormous length of fabric without doublechecking the measurements and ended up spoiling the piece, so that she had to cut the rest with extra care in order to have enough fabric to finish. Mami spent three quarters of an hour showing pattern samples to a customer, and the woman finally settled on the design she had admired in the first place. And the phone kept ringing. Finally, one sofa was completed, and Papi and Joey loaded it into the truck.

"Is there anything else to do before I get ready to go to Trumbull?" Luisa asked.

"No," Mami said, "but I've never seen you this excited about going to the shopping center with Mary Beth."

Ignoring Mami, Luisa sped through a hot shower, and washed and blow-dried her hair. She had spent two hours on the phone with Mary Beth and Karen, deciding what to wear. They had settled on corduroy pants and a sweater, the most Trumbull sort of outfit. Luisa had a pretty, rose-colored sweater Abuela had knit for her last Christmas. She knew that pink was becoming on her, with her olive-gold coloring. She was about to put on some mascara and blush, when she remembered what Tom had said. Besides, it was better luck not to try too hard.

Joey returned from the delivery all hot and sweaty, but

Luisa was lying in wait for him. If he got started on one of his showers, that would be it for the afternoon.

"Okay," he said, "but you'd better tell old Mary Beth to wear a gas mask." He took an appreciative whiff of his perspiration-stained armpits.

"What's up in Trumbull?" Joey asked, as he started the van and backed carefully out of the narrow driveway.

"Nothing," Luisa answered, and smiled. Joey didn't ask anything else.

When they arrived at Mary Beth's, Luisa joined her in the back of the van. That was the one good thing about being in the reupholstery business: The truck was always filled with sofas and chairs, so you could ride around comfortably even in the back. Of course, if you didn't have a reupholstery business in the first place, you might have a car to ride in instead, like everyone else. Luisa eased into a dignified Wedgewood-blue wing-back chair, and Mary Beth sprawled out on an old, overstuffed sofa. They exchanged a look of steadfast determination.

At the mall they headed straight for the snack bar. While fortifying themselves with french fries and Cokes, they pored over Mary Beth's map of Trumbull. They had already marked their intended route earlier in the week. They would have a lot of walking to do, but they would have covered every street in Trumbull when they were finished.

Luisa drowned the last french fry in catsup. "Maybe Karen is right, and this is just a wild goose chase," she said.

"Look," Mary Beth asked, "do you want to see him again or not?"

"I do."

"Then this is the only way."

They started walking. It was a crisp, bright-blue October day, and the streets were thick with colored leaves. There were more trees in two Trumbull blocks than in half of Bridgeport. Lots of fathers were out raking, and teen-age kids, but not him.

"I knew he wouldn't be raking leaves," Luisa said. "He's not the type."

There were cars in almost every driveway, but no blue Mustangs. Luisa was glad she had an older brother who was crazy about cars. Otherwise, she might not have known it was a Mustang she was looking for. A lot of people, like Mary Beth, wouldn't know a Mustang from a Cougar. They had seen two blue Cougars.

Suddenly, a blue Mustang passed them, going fast, and disappeared around the corner. Luisa knew, the way she knew that he wasn't the leaf-raking type, that he drove fast. He hadn't exactly been driving the speed limit when he almost ran her over on East Main Street. She broke into a run. Mary Beth followed, and they sprinted around the corner just in time to see the blue Mustang turn onto a side street three blocks up.

"My side hurts," Mary Beth gasped, and Luisa slowed to a walk. You couldn't outrun a speeding car.

"Is it him?" Mary Beth panted, pushing her unruly reddish curls back from her perspiring face. Both her braids had come undone.

"I don't know," Luisa said. "I couldn't see the driver—the car went by so fast. But that was just the way he drives. Come on, let's see where the car turned off."

The side street was a wide, pleasant avenue with a generous strip of lawn between the sidewalks and the road. Two rows of stately oak trees, mostly bare now, but with a few crimson leaves still fluttering against the brilliant blue sky, almost formed an arch overhead. Luisa knew it was his street. This was where he belonged. She compared the trim green bags of raked leaves lining the curb with the battered garbage cans on Tilden Street.

"Look!" Mary Beth cried. "In front of the stone house with the gingerbread trim—is that the blue car?"

There, where Mary Beth was pointing, was a blue Mustang.

"What do we do now?" Luisa whispered, suddenly afraid.

"We just casually saunter by and see who lives there."

"What if he's there?"

"Then you turn on your charm and I disappear."

He wasn't there, but a pleasant-looking, middle-aged woman—slim, wearing an aqua pantsuit, with her hair cropped becomingly short—was unloading a bag of groceries from the trunk.

"His mother," Mary Beth hissed.

The woman with the groceries saw the girls hesitate in front of the house and gave them a friendly smile. "Are you girls looking for somebody?" she called out.

"We're looking for the Petrowskis," Mary Beth said, and Luisa stifled a giggle. Mr. Petrowski was the janitor at Our Lady of the Mountains.

"I don't know any family by that name," the woman said. "Are you sure they live on Moore Street?"

"I think so," Mary Beth said. She looked at Luisa for support.

"That's a nice car," Luisa said. It was all she could think of.

"My son's just wild about it," the woman said.

Son. My son. Luisa felt weak.

"It's all I can do to tear him away from it so I can make

a run to the store. He just got his license," she explained. "Do you girls drive?"

"Not yet," Mary Beth answered.

"But soon," Luisa added.

They waited.

"Well, I hope you find the people you were looking for, the Petrov—"

"The Petrowskis," Mary Beth said. "Thank you."

The woman smiled again and picked up a second bag of groceries.

"Is your son at home?" Luisa blurted out.

His mother looked a little surprised, but not displeased. Luisa figured she must be used to lots of girls having a crush on her son.

"He's right upstairs. Harold!" she called, her eyes twinkling.

Immediately, a fat, round-shouldered boy with thick, black-framed glasses walked through the front door, a chocolate Devil Dog in one hand and a can of Dr. Pepper in the other.

He gave Luisa and Mary Beth a blank stare. Their look at him was one of numb horror.

"These young ladies were admiring the Mustang," his mother said.

"It's quite a car," Harold said, and gulped down the rest of the Devil Dog.

"Yes, it's quite a car," Mary Beth echoed. "Well, good-bye, Mrs. . . ."

"Barrett," Harold's mother said.

"Good-bye, Harold." She nudged Luisa.

"Good-bye," Luisa said, and then, although they both meant to walk away slowly, steadily, without looking back, they broke into a run. They ran down to the street where they had first seen the blue Mustang and then kept going, running all the way back to the shopping center.

"Oh, Mary Beth," Luisa moaned, once she had recovered her breath. "Wasn't that perfectly terrible?"

"Actually," Mary Beth said, "I think it was pretty funny." She giggled. Luisa giggled. And then they laughed and laughed, until Luisa's stomach hurt and tears were running down Mary Beth's cheeks.

"Is that the end of Phase One?" Luisa asked, trying not to think of how surprised they must have looked when Harold and his Devil Dog made their grand entrance.

"Certainly not," Mary Beth said. "That was just one blue Mustang. We can't stop until we've tracked down every blue Mustang in Trumbull. If we don't finish today, then we'll come back next week, and the week after that."

Luisa sighed. "I'm not sure anymore. I mean, I'm sure I want to see him, but I think that when I'm meant to see him, I'll see him, and it won't be as a result of some big, organized campaign. It'll be unexpected, like at the Laundromat, or the bowling alley, or the Dunkin' Donuts."

"What is Mr. Superwasp Trumbull going to be doing at the East Side Laundromat?" Mary Beth demanded.

"I don't know," Luisa said. "Washing his clothes. What was he doing on East Main Street in the first place?"

"Lightning," Mary Beth returned, "doesn't strike twice."

CHAPTER

5

"I don't know about you," Luisa said, "but I feel as if I ate those french fries two weeks ago."

"How about ice cream, then?"

"My treat," Luisa offered. "It's the least I can do after you've sprinted all over Trumbull for me, exposing yourself to Harolds and everything. And you know if you ever want me to help track down any guy for you, you just have to say the word."

"I know," Mary Beth said, as they lined up in the ice cream shop for cones. She ordered a double-dip vanilla, and Luisa, a double dip with chocolate ice cream and orange sherbet.

"How about that lifeguard at the Laundromat?" Luisa asked, blending the chocolate and orange together with her tongue. "He's all yours now, since I have the WASP in the blue Mustang."

"No, he's your type, not mine."

"What's your type, then?"

Mary Beth ignored the question. "Phase Two," she said, indicating with her ice cream cone the bulletin board by the cash register, "is to steep ourselves in everything Trumbull: to read the Trumbull news and Trumbull help-wanted and real estate ads. We could even go to mass some Sunday in Trumbull. We could tell our parents that the sisters thought we should visit different parishes."

"He's not Catholic," Luisa reminded her, wishing Mary Beth wouldn't change the subject whenever her own romantic prospects were mentioned. "But—"

She stopped. There, in the middle of the bulletin board, was a poster advertising the Trumbull High School homecoming dance. The dance was scheduled for Saturday, October 17. It was now Saturday, October 17.

"It's tonight," Luisa said. "Of course, how could we have been so stupid? We weren't going to find him hanging around at home on a Saturday afternoon in football season. Not with that body. Not with that sweater. He's playing football. Right now he's at the game. And tonight he's going to be at that dance."

"And," Mary Beth said, "we're going to be at the dance, too. That's Phase Three."

"Will they let us go?"

"Well, what if Joey went to the dance, too, and kind of"— she grimaced—"you know, protected us? My parents might come around then. They think your brother can do no wrong."

"Well, I'll ask him," Luisa said. She knew Joey hated dances. But she also knew that Mary Beth was right. She wasn't going to find this guy by peering into all the garages in Trumbull and then hiding in the bushes whenever she saw a blue Mustang, on the chance that he might come out to claim it. And, really, what if he did? What would she do then? Go ring the doorbell and try to sell him an Our Lady of the Mountains raffle ticket? No, the dance was the only way.

Besides, it wasn't every day that the embodiment of all her dreams, an incredibly good-looking guy who wasn't poor or ethnic or Catholic, drove down East Main Street, right into her life. If she didn't take advantage of this opportunity, would she ever get another chance? She had to go to the dance; that was all there was to it.

Getting there was another question altogether. Mami

and Papi hadn't even liked it when she had gone to one of the nun-chaperoned dances that Our Lady of the Mountains sponsored every spring, where nice Catholic boys from St. Francis of Assisi, all dressed up in hand-me-down suits, arrived in busloads. The dance lasted until eleven, but Papi had made Joey pick her up at ten-thirty. If only she had already had that stupid *quince*. Maybe then her parents would let her participate in normal, American, twentieth-century dating practices. Still, a local dance under Sister Bernice's supervision was one thing, and a dance all the way up in Trumbull was another. It seemed as if it all depended on Joey.

He came to pick them up as soon as they called. They spotted the shabby old van with the big dent on the passenger side as it turned into the parking lot, and ran over to meet him.

"Any luck *shopping?*" Joey asked.

"Well, sort of," Luisa said. "That is, I mean, if you co-operate just a little."

"Doesn't sound good," Joey said. "I smell trouble."

"Luisa and I were thinking," Mary Beth began, "that you might like to go to a dance with us tonight."

"Then you and Luisa," Joey said, "were thinking wrong."

"Oh, please," Luisa said. "It's in Trumbull and we just have to go, and Mami and Papi will never let us go if you don't take us, and they probably won't let us go even then, and nothing in the world has ever been so important to me."

"Why Trumbull?"

"If I tell you, will you take us?"

"If you don't tell me, I won't even consider it."

Luisa looked at Mary Beth helplessly.

"We met a guy," Mary Beth said. "Or rather, Luisa met a guy. He's from Trumbull, and he plays on the football team. Tonight's the homecoming dance. And if she's ever going to see him again, we have to go."

"Trumbull lost twenty-eight to seven today, so I doubt that Mr. Right's going to be in the mood for a celebration. But you've got yourself a deal, if Mami and Papi say it's okay, and if Papi doesn't need the van to go to jai alai. And if both of you—that goes for you, too, Mary Beth—promise to dance with me at least half a dozen times, so I don't have to stand around, looking like a fool in front of those Trumbull blue bloods."

Luisa hoped to find Mami and Papi in a receptive mood. She was relieved to hear Mami singing over the loud music of the kitchen radio: A fat letter had arrived from Papi's brother Carlos in Cuba. Cuban-American mail service was notoriously slow and unreliable, with letters arriving weeks or even months late, if they arrived at all. So Mami and Papi were going out to the diner with Luisa's aunt Consuela and uncle Angel to celebrate.

But as soon as the dance was mentioned, Papi started his usual shouting: He wasn't going to have his only daughter who wasn't even fifteen yet whoring around all over the state.

"Do you know what the Yankee tourists used to call Havana?" he asked Luisa. She knew, but figured she might as well let him go ahead and say it.

"Sin City," he said, "the sin capital of the world. And do you know why they called it that?"

Luisa didn't answer.

"Because the streets were filled with prostitutes, whores, cheap girls with no respect for their fathers and mothers, no respect for themselves. The nice girls weren't out there looking for dates; no, they were home with their parents."

He turned to Mami. "When you were her age, did you go out without a chaperone?"

"Joey's going to the dance with me," Luisa said. "And Mary Beth."

"Mary Beth!" Papi snorted.

"It's just a dance, Ernesto," Mami said then. Luisa was surprised, but she shouldn't have been—Mami usually came around when it really mattered. "The young people here start going to dances earlier than they do in Cuba. I'm sure there will be teachers from the school there. The Trumbull parents wouldn't allow it otherwise."

"I'll make sure nothing happens to her," Joey said.

"You want Luisa to be like the other girls, don't you?" Mami asked.

"No!" Papi said. "That's exactly what I *don't* want."

But at eight o'clock the three of them were on their way to Trumbull. Luisa sat very still in the back of the van, gripping the arms of the wing-back chair until her knuckles turned white. She knew she would see him tonight. But would he have a girl friend? Would he remember her from the accident? What would she say if he asked her where she was from, or what she had been doing on East Main Street that day?

Mary Beth interrupted her thoughts. "What if we run into our friend Harold?"

Luisa knew that Mary Beth meant the question as a joke, but she suddenly became alarmed. What if she *did* run into Harold? He might ask her to dance, and the guy in the blue Mustang would think she was Harold's girl friend. She half wanted to tell Joey to turn around. But then she saw the lights pulsing from the windows of the

Trumbull High School gym and heard the disco music blaring. She couldn't turn back.

"Maybe Harold doesn't go to dances," she said, and added a silent prayer.

Once inside the semi-dark gym, illuminated only by bursting flashes of light that reflected off a mirrored ball, like the kind they had at the New York City discos, Luisa could see he wasn't there. But she didn't panic. He wouldn't come early to a stupid high school dance, like all the eager beavers. He and his friends would drive around for a while, maybe have a few beers—not too many, she hoped—and then drop by. She looked at her watch. It was just eight thirty-five. Maybe by nine. . . .

The dance was so un-Bridgeport and un-Our Lady of the Mountains that she could hardly believe it. Everyone was white, except for a handful of black kids dancing together on one side. Most of the girls were as conservatively dressed as she was—she had changed from cords and a sweater to straight-legged jeans and a velour top—but a few wore blouses that were very low cut and very see-through. They would have absolutely blown Sister Bernice away.

"Excuse me, would you—would you like to dance?"

Luisa turned around, startled. Before her stood not the guy in the blue Mustang, not Harold, but a stranger—a skinny, sandy-haired guy with glasses. He smiled then, and with the smile he looked almost handsome. But how could she dance with someone else when the guy in the blue Mustang might arrive at any minute? Still, you couldn't refuse one boy and then dance with another—that would be so rude.

"Sure," Mary Beth said hesitantly, returning the boy's smile, and they joined the crowd of dancers.

He had been talking to Mary Beth! Guys hardly ever asked Mary Beth to dance, at least not when Luisa or Karen was around. It wasn't that Mary Beth wasn't pretty, because she was, with her curly reddish-brown hair and large blue eyes. But she didn't experiment with the forbidden eyeshadow or lipstick the way Luisa and Karen did, and she persisted in wearing her hair in the same chunky braids she had worn since grade school. Even though she had enough baby-sitting money to buy herself something new, she still wore her sisters' hand-me-downs. And, to make matters worse, as soon as there was a guy around, except for Tom or Joey, Mary Beth stopped talking and just sat like a lump, staring down at the floor. At the Our Lady dance, only two boys had managed to find her in a corner behind the bleachers and ask her to dance. And they had both been—well, creeps.

But this new guy looked promising. He wasn't the WASP in the blue Mustang or anything, but he was here, in the flesh, dancing with Mary Beth. And the WASP in the blue Mustang was nowhere in sight.

Joey came up behind her. "May I have the honor of this dance?" he asked with a bow. Casting a backward glance at the door of the gym, Luisa curtsied, and they started to dance.

Luisa wouldn't have minded if the guy in the blue Mustang thought she was with Joey. He was so good-looking, and even though he hated dances, he loved to dance. She loved to dance, too, and followed him effortlessly in all sorts of disco steps, swinging and dipping back and forth, hardly aware of her feet and the movements they were executing.

They had practiced together at home, but only when Papi wasn't around. Papi had smashed a whole pile of

Luisa's records one night, when he heard "Love to Love You, Baby." If he ever again heard a song like that on her stereo, he threatened, he would send her to a convent in Spain.

Luisa realized that a group of kids was watching them, but she didn't feel shy. She never felt shy when she was dancing. She added a couple of flourishes for their benefit, and at one point Joey even picked her up and whirled her around. But suddenly, as Joey set her gracefully on her feet again, she saw him there, part of the admiring crowd, the guy with the blue Mustang.

The music stopped. Joey headed for the ice chest filled with sodas, and Luisa, after a moment's hesitation, joined Mary Beth and her partner. She hated to interrupt Mary Beth's first tête-à-tête with a nice-looking guy, but she couldn't go through this alone, she just couldn't. Mary Beth would understand.

"He's here," she murmured, nodding in his direction. And then, as she went through the motions of an introduction to Doug, she stole her first good look at him. He was wearing the same Trumbull letter sweater he had worn the other day, and he was even better looking than she remembered.

He was standing with a couple of other guys in letter sweaters, and laughing. One of them looked at her. She gave what she hoped was a suggestive smile, then modestly looked away. When she glanced back, he was looking at her, too. First he looked at her the way his friend had, slowly sizing up a strange female in Trumbull territory. But then he looked puzzled, and Luisa could tell he was trying to remember where he had seen her before. She shot him an encouraging smile. He smiled apologetically, and then recognition dawned. He walked across the gym to her, while the band played "You'll Never Find Another Love Like Mine."

"How are your knees?" he asked. Before she could answer, he went on, "You'd never believe how you scared me, running right in front of the car like that. I thought for sure I wouldn't be able to stop."

"I'm okay," Luisa said. The music was so loud that he had to bend his head toward hers to hear her. "I've been looking both ways now: Cross on the green and not in between."

"That's great," he said. "All that grade-school stuff gets drummed into our heads, and then what do we do? We walk right into the middle of heavy traffic just like we were from another planet."

They looked at each other.

"Well," he said. "You may not know how to cross streets by yourself, but you sure know how to dance."

"Thanks," Luisa said. "I thought maybe it looked like we were showing off."

"Who's the guy?"

Luisa decided she might as well be honest. She didn't think he was the sort to thrive on competition.

"My brother," she confessed.

"Figures," he said. "He looks like he'd be good on the team. We could sure use some help on defense. But, hey, you're some athlete yourself, jogging way the hell over to Bridgeport. That's a good few miles from here. How long have you been running?"

"Pretty long," Luisa said. Thank goodness she had been jogging that afternoon, and that she had had the presence of mind to leave the telltale bag of bananas on the sidewalk behind her!

He had mentioned the team. She knew she should

make some comment about the afternoon's defeat, to let him know she knew all about it and was interested. Also, that she thought he was wonderful even though his team had been beaten—what was the score again?—28 to something. But by whom? And what was she going to say about it?

A fast song began. "What do you say we dance?" he asked. Luisa sighed with relief. Dancing was so much easier than talking. "I don't know any of the fancy steps your brother does, though," he said, a little belligerently.

"That's okay," Luisa said, and he casually put his arm around her shoulder as he cocked his head toward her.

"I said, that's okay," she repeated, a little more loudly. Then he took her by the hand and led her out to the dance floor.

CHAPTER

6
They danced together for four songs. He wasn't much of a dancer, Luisa acknowledged with a fond smile. Little of his athletic grace carried over to the dance floor, and he moved his muscular body self-consciously, shifting his weight monotonously from one foot to the other in time—more or less—to the driving disco music. Then the band began a slow number and he gathered her in his arms. His idea of slow-dancing was to swallow his partner in a close embrace and slowly rock back and forth. Luisa had never before danced like that with a guy. Until tonight her only dancing experiences had been at home with Joey, with other relatives at weddings, and with the boys from St. Francis of Assisi. She couldn't even imagine what the nuns would have said if she had danced with the boys from St. Francis the way she was dancing with Travis.

Fast music was played again. "Hey," he said. "I've got my car outside. You remember, the famous implement of destruction. How about going out for something to eat? I've had about all I can take of this crazy dance."

"I'd love to," she began, wanting to leave the dance with Travis more than anything in the world. Every time she had glanced over Travis's shoulder at her brother, she had found him watching her. All Joey really needed was a big hooked nose and a black habit, and he could double for Sister Bernice. But she knew she needed Joey's cooperation if she was going to see Travis again. She couldn't afford to make him angry. "I wish I could," she told Travis, "but my brother would never let me."

"You're kidding! Let me talk to this guy!" he said, with

a mock threatening air. But he seemed genuinely bothered, maybe even a little annoyed.

Luisa didn't want Travis talking to Joey. She couldn't count on Joey, at least not without further coaching, and maybe not even then, not to give her away. It would be just like Joey to say, "It's getting late. We really ought to pile into the furniture van and head back to East Main Street."

"You don't know my brother," she said. "Talking to him won't do any good."

"Come on," he coaxed. "How about a little ride, just around the block? We'll be back before big brother even notices that you're gone."

"Will we be back by eleven?" she asked, her resolve rapidly weakening.

"Scout's honor." He grinned, and she gave in.

Joey was dancing with Mary Beth on the other side of the gym. He had his back to her. "Let's go," she said quickly, before she could change her mind.

It was cold in the parking lot, cold enough for Luisa to see her breath clouding in the light from the streetlamps. She really should have stopped at the cloakroom for her jacket, but she hated that cheap old thing, made of a stiff maroon-plaid synthetic she had seen on two thousand East Side Puerto Ricans. But then Travis draped his letter sweater, still warm from his body heat, over her shoulders. It hung almost to her knees. "You need to grow," he kidded.

He opened the door of the blue Mustang for her, and, still shivering, she slid into the cold bucket seat. He started the engine and looked over at her.

"You're still cold," he observed. "Damn bucket seats." He pulled her to him across the console and held her close, closer even than he had during the dance, and rubbed her back and shoulders slowly. Luisa knew he was going to kiss her. No one had ever kissed her before, but she didn't want him to know that. She tried to summon up all she knew about kissing. Your eyes should be closed, so that you don't stare at each other the whole time, eyeball to eyeball. But you shouldn't close them too soon and purse your lips expectantly, the way Scarlett O'Hara did when Rhett Butler brought her the green silk bonnet. Your mouth should be moist, but not slobbery. She furtively licked her lips.

And then his mouth was on hers, and she had no time to think of anything else.

She wasn't sure that she liked it, because he forced his tongue between her lips and partway down her throat, so that she almost choked. But she guessed that you got used to it, and maybe even learned to enjoy it.

He slid his hand under her velour pullover and she moved away, frightened. "Please don't," she said, hoping he would stop, and that she would be able to keep on saying no to him if he didn't. Sister Marguerita, who taught health, said that boys liked and respected you more if you told them no. They knew the difference between girls who were nice and girls who weren't, and while they would try to go as far as they could with a girl who wasn't nice, they would marry only nice girls. But did that go for non-Catholic boys as well? And how much did Sister Marguerita know about boys, anyway? Why would they try to feel your breasts if they didn't want you to let them? None of it made any sense to her.

To her surprise and immense relief, Travis moved his hand. "Tell me if I go too fast for you," he murmured.

Luisa knew she was going to have to tell him enough

lies, so she might as well be honest about something. Besides, she just couldn't let him touch her that way. Not yet, at least.

"I'm not used to—used to being with a guy like this," she stammered.

"Someone who dances the way you do?" he asked. "Really?"

"Really."

He seemed disappointed but then kissed her again, longer than before.

"I can wait for a while," he told her. "Don't be afraid of me."

After the next kiss Luisa said, "We should be going back. Joey and Mary Beth will have sent out a search party."

"Right-o, Cinderella," he said. "We certainly don't want you turning into a pumpkin."

The music was still blaring inside the gym. Right away Luisa spotted Joey and Mary Beth looking intently through the dancing crowd. Evidently, her disappearance had not gone unnoticed. Doug was with them—that, at least, was nice.

"My brother and my friend are looking for me," she said. But she stayed hidden in the crowd by the door. She didn't know how she would be able to handle her farewell to Travis with the three of them staring at her.

"Okay, okay," he said. "So when do I see you again?"

Then it came to her, the wonderful idea.

"I don't know. I mean, I really want to see you again, but—well, my parents are super-strict. They fuss over me ten thousand times more than my brother does. So I think they'd freak out if you came to my house, or anything like that."

"Where do you live, anyway?" he asked.

"In Weston," Luisa lied hastily.

"Weston," he echoed, raising his eyebrows. "Your folks must not be hurting."

"They do okay," Luisa said, wishing she had thought of a less swank location.

"How are they about phone calls? Are men allowed to talk to their precious daughter by means of that most handy invention, the telephone?"

Luisa thought quickly. No, she couldn't risk having Mami shout into the receiver, "¿Halo? ¿Halo? ¿Quién es?"

"It'd probably be better if you didn't," she said. "I know it sounds crazy. I could call you, if you don't think that's a bad idea. Some guys don't like it if girls call them." She suspected that Travis was one of those guys.

"*This* guy would like it if *this* girl called him. But maybe you should hang up if my mom answers. She's pretty old-fashioned. Do you have a scrap of paper?"

Luisa shook her head.

"Well, the number's in the phone book. Travis Blaine— well, my father is Michael—on Elm Street."

"Got it," she said.

He brushed her lips lightly with his. "Take it easy."

It wasn't a declaration of undying love, but Luisa felt her heart skip a beat at that parting "Take it easy": so cool, casual, self-assured, but a little bit caring, too.

The instant she got home from mass the next morning, Luisa took the phone into the bathroom and called Mary Beth.

"I can't talk now," she whispered. "Papi's still not talking to us because he heard us come in at a quarter to twelve. He says I can't go to a dance again till I'm twenty-one. But listen, I have to get some bread at the bakery. Can you meet me there in half an hour?"

"Sure," Mary Beth answered. "But did he kiss you? Are you going to see him again?"

"I have to go," Luisa said, "but the answers are yes and yes."

When Luisa arrived at Mr. Alfonso's bakery, Mary Beth was already there, perched on her bike in the parking lot.

"How was it, the first kiss?" she demanded.

"It was," Luisa said, "absolutely and in every way perfect. Did you have a good time with Doug?"

"Sure," Mary Beth said, maddeningly noncommittal. "But I was thinking about you and Travis the whole time. You're right, he *is* better looking than Robert Redford. Did he french kiss?"

"I'll say!" Luisa exclaimed with a grimace, forgetting that the kiss had been described as in every way perfect.

"You didn't like it?"

"Of course I liked it. It just takes some getting used to. It was better, really, after the first couple of times."

"He didn't try anything else, did he?" Mary Beth asked, just as Luisa was hoping she wouldn't.

She lowered her voice, although the practically deserted parking lot in front of the bakery could hardly have concealed any eavesdroppers. "He tried, but he stopped when I asked him to."

Mary Beth didn't say anything, waiting for the details that were sure to be forthcoming.

"He put his hand under my sweater."

"Are you going to tell Father McCarthy in confession?"

"Of course not. And, Mary Beth, if you dare tell anyone—"

"You know I won't. But I still think you should tell Father McCarthy, or at least Sister Marguerita. Well, maybe not Sister Marguerita. But somebody. I mean, I really think it would make you feel better—"

"I *feel* perfectly fine. And besides, it isn't even wrong."

Mary Beth looked doubtful.

"It isn't. You can't tell me you really believe you'll go to hell if you let someone kiss you before you get married. Didn't Doug even try to kiss you?" The question sounded so cruel that Luisa felt somehow even angrier: Mary Beth had no business provoking her into being mean.

"We're not talking about kissing. And, no, I don't think you'll go to hell because someone tried to feel you up. But I do think it's wrong to—well, I think it's wrong to let someone put his hands all over you, unless you're really in love."

"But I am."

"Is he?"

"Yes," Luisa said, knowing she wasn't fooling anyone. But she had to defend herself against Mary Beth—not that Mary Beth was saying anything Luisa hadn't already said to herself. She didn't know if what she had done in the car was right or wrong; she did know that it had made her frightened and uncomfortable. But she also knew that Sister Marguerita had her facts all wrong. Guys—that is, guys like Travis—didn't like prudes. And Luisa had never wanted anything as much as she wanted Travis to like her.

"Listen, Mary Beth, please, let's not fight. You're my best friend." Why did she suddenly feel like crying? "You have to understand how much I want him to be in love with me, too, even if he isn't, yet. And I know that if I don't kiss him or whatever, there are a million girls like me who'll kiss him instead."

"Not like you. Not as pretty as you, or as much fun to be with. And that's why you don't have to let him do anything you don't want him to."

Luisa felt embarrassed by Mary Beth's loyalty, and ashamed.

"It's just that—there are things that aren't wrong if you love somebody." Was she trying to convince Mary Beth or herself? She didn't know what else to say.

"So this is Phase Four," Mary Beth said, helping her out.

"Phase Four?"

"Luisa in love."

CHAPTER

7

Luisa wanted to call Travis on Monday and Tuesday, but she didn't. She made herself wait. She knew he couldn't call her; he didn't even know her last name or where she lived. Besides, she had made such a point of asking him not to. But she still had daydreams of his tracking her down—after all, she had tracked him down after a chance five-minute encounter—and defying her parents' wrath to come see her, here, three doors down from the bar, on a street littered with empty liquor bottles. He would love her even though she lived on the East Side and her parents didn't speak English very well, and he would take her away from all this. Every time the doorbell rang, her heart beat faster, expecting it to be him.

And the doorbell rang constantly. Customers came by all evening, threading their way rather grandly, Luisa thought, through the cluttered living room to the back shop—or "chop," as Mami pronounced it when she spoke English to them. When Luisa was introduced to the politely condescending customers, she felt even sorrier for her brother than for herself. At least she didn't have to see them in their own homes. Joey had to walk through plush, white-carpeted entrance foyers in his mended, sweaty old work clothes on pickups and deliveries with Papi. But Joey didn't seem to mind, and when the customers came by, he'd just make pleasant conversation with them about the weather or sports.

There were plenty of other interruptions, too. Luisa's aunt Consuela, Mami's sister, and her wheeling-dealing husband, Angel, made stops at Tilden Street on the way to and from their seven-year-old daughter Karina's dancing school. The Martinezes from upstairs clattered down the noisy wooden staircase to borrow odd cups of flour and sugar, which they never returned. The Castilian mechanic who worked on the van whenever it had trouble—which was practically all the time—hung around after repairs for a beer or two—or three—with Papi. Roberto, Anna, and Bobby stopped by to tempt Papi to jai alai now that the World Series was over. The Yankees had lost, and Tom came over to offer his condolences.

"It just goes to show," he said, "that the Yankees can buy the best players in the game, but that doesn't mean they can play baseball."

Tom had a part-time job evenings and weekends, delivering pizzas for Victor's Pizzeria. He and Joey both wanted to save something for college next year. They were applying for scholarships to the University of Connecticut up in Storrs, but if that didn't work out they'd have to go part time to nearby Housatonic Community College.

Whenever Tom got off work early, he would head straight for the Ruizes' with leftover pizza. He sure picked a good place to get rid of anything fattening, Luisa told herself, comparing Mami with the slim woman in the aqua pantsuit whom she still thought of as Travis's mother.

Tuesday evening the pizza was extra cheese with mushrooms and pepperoni, and even Luisa had a slice. She would just skip lunch tomorrow, that was all, and, anyway, she was sure not to see anybody until the weekend.

"This one lady," Tom said, putting his sturdy boots up on the battered coffee table and reaching for another slice of pizza, "ordered five whole medium pizzas and two slices."

"Were the slices a different kind of pizza?"

"Nope. All extra cheese." He laughed. "But she gave

me a three-dollar tip, so I wasn't about to hassle her with any questions."

"Do you get tips from most people?" Joey asked.

"About half and half. It depends on how much beer they've had—or what they've been smoking—before they call out for their pies. It's not bad though, because Victor's pretty decent about money. I made about fifteen, twenty bucks tonight. Victor needs someone else, by the way, so if you're interested, just let me know. I'm sure Victor would hire anybody I told him was all right."

Joey didn't say anything, but Papi did.

"José no need a job," Papi said in English. "He already have a job. Right, José?"

Joey wiped his mouth with the back of his hand, ignoring the napkin Mami handed him.

"If I worked at Victor's," he said unexpectedly, "I could still give you a hand with the deliveries when I had time off."

Papi looked as if Joey had hit him, and then he exploded. "Your mother and I, we have gave you everything!" he shouted. "We give you to eat and your clothes and this house for live in. I work hard, ten hour, twelve hour a day and I no complain. But what do I get? That's right, what do I get? My son leave his father and go to work for a stranger!"

"I told you I'd still help when I could," Joey said. Mami shook her head warningly at him. She hated it so when Joey and Papi fought.

" 'When I could! When I could'!" Papi mimicked. "You help this other guy when he want you to and your own Papi you help when you could." He got up out of his chair. "Maybe I quit the business, too, hey? Maybe I go work for some other family and help out here when I could!" He stormed out of the house. Then they heard the van's engine cough twice and start up.

"Why you have to make your father unhappy?" Mami asked, stroking Joey's hair.

"I can't believe it," he said, jerking his head away. "He should be happy that I want to get a job, and that I'm not out robbing grocery stores like half the guys around here."

"But we give you money, your Papi and I, for the school and for to spend. We want, but we no can give you more."

"You don't understand," Joey said. "That's just the whole point. I don't want you and Papi to give me money. I'm seventeen and I don't want or need an allowance like you'd give a five-year-old. I want to work for an hour and get paid for an hour, and I want the money in a check at the end of the week."

"Don't worry about it," Tom advised. "Victor always needs someone. Just wait it out for a while. Your dad'll come around."

"Yeah," Joey said. "Maybe in twenty years."

"How about a beer, yes, José? Tom?"

"I'm going for a walk," Joey said, almost rudely. He left, as Papi had, without a coat.

"I'll take you up on that beer," Tom said, smiling at Mami sympathetically. When Mami, winking back tears, had bustled into the kitchen, he exchanged looks with Luisa.

"Whew!" he whistled. "Next time I'll keep my big mouth shut."

"It wasn't your fault," Luisa told him. "You thought you were in the United States, in the 1970s. How were you supposed to know that this is really Cuba, before the revolution?"

"Well, don't be too hard on your parents. It takes people a long time to adjust to a new culture. You know that."

"Ten years *is* a long time," Luisa said.

Mami brought in Tom's beer. She had poured it out of the can into a large Mexican beer mug that said "South of the Border" on it and showed a toreador holding out a red cape in front of a bull. Luisa knew that Mami had served the beer in that mug because she thought it was elegant, and Luisa glared at her. Beer wasn't elegant, and even if beer was, the "South of the Border" mug wasn't.

Smiling now, Mami handed Tom the cable TV bulletin. "You want?" she asked.

"Can't you see we're trying to talk?" Luisa said in Spanish, and, still smiling, Mami went back to the kitchen.

"I would think that in ten years people could learn to speak real English," Luisa continued. "And figure out that not everyone in the universe thinks the way people in Cuba did."

"But look at your parents. They took correspondence courses in furniture reupholstering so they could start their own business. They speak English well enough to deal with their customers. And they're not on welfare, or taking any special favors from anyone."

"I get financial aid at Our Lady of the Mountains," Luisa pointed out.

"That's just because they needed a pro-makeup agitator to stir up some dissent in the student body. How's the campaign going?"

"Okay, I guess. I've been kind of busy."

"Your brother told me that some guy in Trumbull has the hots for you."

Luisa was surprised. She didn't think that Joey and Tom ever talked about her when she wasn't around.

"I guess so. At least, I hope so."

"First love." He sighed theatrically, but Luisa knew he wasn't really making fun of her. "All I can say is that he'd better be something special."

"He is," Luisa said.

Tom shrugged on his jacket and got ready to pick up his aunt from work. But he looked troubled about something. Probably, Luisa thought, the quarrel between Joey and Papi was still bothering him. "Thanks for the beer," he called to Mami in the kitchen, and then, as he turned to leave, he took Luisa's chin in his hand and tilted her face up to his. He looked at her for a moment. "Take it easy, will you," he finally said, and then rumpled her hair in his big-brotherly way.

Abuela, Abuelo, and Roberto were coming in as Tom was going out. Roberto had taken them with him to jai alai, and Abuela was beside herself with excitement. "He won two hundred and fifty dollars!" she repeated several times in amazement.

"Did you win any money, Abuela?" Luisa asked, making room for her grandmother beside her on the sofa.

"Oh, no, I bet on two games and I lost on two games, just two dollars each time, but Roberto won two hundred and fifty! Two hundred and fifty dollars!"

"A couple more lucky nights," Roberto boasted, "and I can treat my favorite goddaughter to the biggest, most splendid *quince* Bridgeport has ever seen."

At the mention of the word *quince*, Abuela stopped her delighted exclamations and started moaning.

"I'll call tomorrow," Mami promised, coming out of the kitchen with beer, a long loaf of Spanish bread, and several packages of cold cuts. "We'll get the Cuban Club's own little band to play. Everyone likes dancing to their music. And I think one of our customers does engraving—he will give me a good price on the invitations. So everything will be settled."

"She needs a dress," Abuela continued, not a bit reassured by Mami's plans.

"Then we'll go to New York with Angel on Saturday, you, Luisa, and me. To the place where he got José the three-piece suit for sixty dollars. It would have cost a hundred and fifty, two hundred off the rack in one of the fancy department stores. 'For you, a friend of Angel's,' the man told us, 'we have a special price.' "

Luisa groaned inwardly. She hated buying her clothes from that warehouse, or whatever it was. She didn't care if they had to pay twice as much for the identical suit or dress somewhere else. It would be worth it to have private dressing rooms and no one jabbering away at you in Spanish the whole time. Besides, she needed her weekends now—now that she had met Travis.

"I think I'm going to be busy this weekend," she said. "I won't have time to go to New York."

But when Abuela shot her a look of misery, Luisa relented. "Maybe next weekend, though. I think I might be free then."

"Oh, did I tell you? We got pictures of Teresa's *quince*. They came in the mail last Saturday," Mami said, rummaging through the untidy pile of letters and papers on the coffee table for the fat envelope from Cuba.

Teresa was Luisa's cousin, the daughter of her father's brother Carlos, who had chosen to remain in Cuba. Luisa still hadn't forgotten how she had felt when her parents told her, the morning they finally heard that their turn had come for one of the twice-daily flights to Miami, that she would have only half an hour to tell Teresa good-bye.

"Will I ever see her again?" she had asked Papi. "If there is another revolution, to overthrow Castro this time," Papi had said. "Or if that no-good, Commie brother of mine ever comes to his senses." The two little girls had kissed and cried, and Luisa had left Teresa all the clothes and toys and dolls that she couldn't take with her.

Abuela examined the photographs eagerly, and although Luisa had already spent a good while looking at them, she, too, crowded close to see them again. Teresa looked so happy in the pictures, in her pink voile dress with puffed sleeves. They had been penpals for the ten years they had been apart, but still, there was so much you couldn't say in a letter. Luisa wondered what Teresa was really like now, and if that was the way she would have been if they, too, had stayed behind in Cuba. It seemed to Luisa just now that everything would have been so much easier there—Joey would have worked in the sugar mill the way Papi and Abuelo had. There wouldn't have been any reupholstery shop or Victor's pizzeria. And there wouldn't have been any super-WASP Travis, riding down East Main Street into her dreams. Everybody would have spoken Spanish there, and, too, with the way Castro was trying to change things, there might not have been so much difference between the East Sides and the Trumbulls.

"So pretty." Abuela sighed. "So very, very pretty."

Joey came in. He was smiling, but he looked very determined. A few minutes later the van pulled into the driveway, and Papi brought a sack full of groceries into the house.

"Who wants ice cream?" he asked, unpacking two half-gallon containers.

Mami and Luisa got out bowls and spoons, and they all

attacked the butter pecan. It was twelve-thirty before everyone had finally gone home. Luisa noticed that Joey and Papi hadn't said anything to each other since coming in. And they went to bed without saying good night.

CHAPTER

8

The *quince* was going to end up costing more than Mami and Abuela had expected. A hundred dollars to rent out the Cuban Club. Two hundred dollars for the band. Ten dollars apiece for every guest invited, and, of course, nobody had as many friends and relatives as the Ruiz family did. Luisa, for one, didn't know how they were going to pay for it all and save any money to help send Joey away to college. Papi still earned most of his money on the day shift at American Consolidated Can, while Mami ran the fledgling reupholstery business pretty much by herself. But even with two incomes, they never seemed to have any money. Luisa had decided that it must all go into pork roasts, fried bananas, and flan. And now, *quinces.*

"We could just skip it, you know," she suggested the following evening, but Mami and Abuela ignored her and kept adding their columns of figures.

"You tell your brother," Mami said, "that he better not go leaving your Papi and me now, when we need him to work for your *quince.*"

Well, if they had wanted to make Luisa feel miserable and guilty, they succeeded. She didn't want Joey to feel he couldn't take the job at Victor's because of her and the party she didn't even want. He and Papi still weren't speaking after the scene last night. Each was waiting for the other to give in and admit he was wrong. Luisa had a feeling they would have a long wait.

"We can borrow some money from Consuela and Angel, I think, and, of course, from Roberto," Mami said, sticking her pencil in between two curlers. "And I think we should all go to the jai alai right now. I feel lucky.

61

Who knows, maybe we'll win just one trifecta and poof
Luisa's *quince* will be all paid."

Luisa really did like going to jai alai. She liked the ex
citement of sitting high in the great arena with everyone
around her frantically cheering for the teams on which
they had wagered their two or three—or more—dollars
Papa would place bets for her and it wasn't unusual to
win enough to buy a blouse or at least some nail polish
but she never took more with her than she was willing to
lose. She knew there were a few Robertos who had made
their fortunes at jai alai, but she herself usually barely
broke even. And some people, like the Portuguese man
who worked at the factory with Papi, lost everything. Ra
had just put a down payment on a house with his jai ala
winnings, when he started losing. After a while the bank
took the house away from him because he couldn't pay
the mortgage.

When Mami finally got off the phone, the party con
sisted of Luisa, Mami, Papi, Joey, Roberto, Anna, and
Tom. Mami had told Luisa she could invite Mary Beth
but Luisa knew Mary Beth wouldn't be able to go—her
parents didn't let her go out on school nights, and they
didn't approve of jai alai, either. They thought that all
gambling that wasn't bingo was sinful. But they went to
bingo as religiously as they went to mass.

Luisa called her anyway, just in case. Besides, she felt
guilty because she hadn't called Mary Beth or Karen since
the weekend. Karen really didn't know anything about
the dance at Trumbull, although she had plied Luisa with
questions on Monday morning. All she knew was that the
two WBM patrol members had ended up abandoning
their walking tour of Trumbull in favor of the homecom
ing dance; Luisa had found Travis at the dance, and
danced with him a few times, and wasn't sure if she

would see him again. Luisa didn't know exactly why she couldn't tell Karen more. Karen hadn't been very enthusiastic about the search for Travis in the first place. Luisa had a feeling Karen might not be any more enthusiastic now that he had been found.

"Have you called him yet?" Mary Beth asked, as soon as she picked up the phone.

"No, I thought I'd try to wait until tomorrow."

"That's cutting it kind of close for the weekend, I'd say. Guys like that don't sit around forever, waiting for some girl they hardly know to call."

"I know. You're right. I just feel that I've been such an eager beaver all along. I don't want to make him think I'm chasing him."

"But he doesn't even know about any of that. He has no idea that we went door-to-door in Trumbull looking for blue Mustangs—"

"And he's never going to know, either. But, anyway, I'll call him tomorrow. Right at eight. I really will. What about Doug? Have you heard anything from him?"

"No," Mary Beth said, and Luisa wished she hadn't asked.

"Maybe he'll call tonight."

"I don't think so. He didn't ask for my number or anything."

"It's in the phone book, though."

"Listen, Luisa, he isn't going to call. I'm not like you. Boys don't call me."

"Mary Beth—"

"I don't mind, believe me. I have a better time just scheming for you, I really do. We're a team: You're beautiful and I'm brilliant—"

"What's Karen?"

"Karen's . . . sophisticated."

"I'd rather be sophisticated than beautiful, and, be-sides, I'm not beautiful."

"Yeah, yeah, tell me about it. Better yet, tell Travis about it."

"So you're not coming to jai alai?"

"No. *Tengo que estudiar español. Hasta mañana.*"

"*Hasta mañana.*" Luisa heard Mary Beth hang up, but she just laid the receiver on the edge of the sink and stood for a moment looking at it. She didn't want to call Travis tomorrow at eight—she was afraid to call him. The dance seemed like a dream now—it had been too perfect, too close to all her wildest fantasies. Dreams came true sometimes, but not so soon, not so easily. What if she called him and found he didn't even remember the dance and how he had pulled her close to him out in the high school parking lot and kissed her? Or what if he remem-bered, but didn't feel the same way anymore? Would he tell her so, or would he make up excuses about why he couldn't see her that weekend, or the next weekend, or the weekend after that?

Receiver in hand, she unlocked the bathroom door. She was doubly glad she was going to jai alai tonight. She wouldn't have to jump every time she heard the doorbell or the telephone, or be tempted to break her vow and call him earlier, if only to get the terrible disappointment over with. But, no, she could wait. She would call him tomorrow, just as she had told Mary Beth she would. To-morrow at eight. She hesitated for a second, then re-placed the receiver in its hook.

Papi and Mami rode to the fronton in the van, and Tom, Joey, and Luisa piled into the backseat of Roberto and Anna's car. Anna had just gotten her hair done that afternoon, and she looked especially young and pretty. Anna had probably had her share of romance before she married Roberto. Maybe Luisa should try to ask her advice about the Travis situation.

"Guess who has a girl friend? Bobby!" Anna said in a single breath. "It's the little girl across the street, and Roberto and I think it's so cute. She's in the first grade with him, and I keep asking him if he is trying to make Karina jealous." Karina was Consuela and Angel's little girl, and Anna had matchmaking fantasies involving the two children. "And he said, no, Karina is marrying Larry!"

"That *is* cute," Luisa said, deciding she wouldn't talk to Anna about Travis, after all.

"Are you all set for jai alai?" Roberto asked them. "Have you said the jai alai prayer?"

"What prayer?" Tom asked.

"Jewishness, Jewishness," Roberto intoned, lifting his hands momentarily from the wheel and folding them in a gesture of supplication, "let me come back with more than I left with."

Luisa didn't like the prayer. Jokes about people's religion always made her uncomfortable, even when she knew they were just jokes. But she laughed, anyway, since Roberto looked over his shoulder to make sure they were all amused.

The jai alai fronton was crowded even on a weeknight, so they ended up parking a quarter of a mile or so away, in a field that had been converted into a parking lot. Joey walked ahead very fast, with his hands wedged tightly into his pockets. Apparently he wasn't in the mood for company, and Anna and Roberto were talking earnestly back at the car, so Luisa and Tom fell into step together.

"The pizza delivery man's night off," he announced.

Luisa smiled.

"So when am I going to meet this Trumbull Romeo?"

"I don't know," Luisa said. She wished everyone wouldn't take it for granted that Travis was interested in her. He probably didn't even remember the dance—or what had happened in his car.

"Has he called to get a date for the weekend yet?"

"I'm supposed to call him," she said.

"Hey, that sounds pretty liberated," he said. "Forget the sexist scene with the girl hanging around all dreamy-eyed by the phone, waiting for him to call."

"It's not like that, though." Luisa didn't know where to begin. "I just didn't want him to know that—well, you know—the East Side and Mami and Papi and the Good Times bar—"

"Wait a minute. You aren't giving this guy half a chance. Why assume right off that he's such a snob as to care about stuff like that?"

"I just get the feeling he is. I don't have any real reasons or anything."

"If you think he's a creep, why bother with him?"

Luisa didn't say anything. She didn't know what to say.

"Okay, okay, spare me the gooey details." He smiled, but Luisa could tell he wasn't satisfied. He was taking all this Travis business more seriously than Joey was, that was for sure.

"Race you," she said, to eliminate the possibility of any more heavy conversation, and tore off across the pavement. Tom sprinted in pursuit and, catching up to her halfway to the fronton, grabbed hold of her hand. They ran the remaining yards together and joined Joey at the ticket booth, panting and laughing, to wait for the others.

Inside the fronton, Roberto picked up programs for everyone, and while the rest of them located their seats, he went to place his first bet on the game that was about to begin: Team 3, Durango and Arrarte, against Team 7, Bebaza and Ondarres. In all there were eight two-player teams listed on the program, to compete against each other round-robin style, until one team accumulated seven points. You could bet on a team to win, place, or show, which was how Luisa usually bet. The returns were small, but the odds of collecting were pretty good and at least, she figured, you came away with something, even if it was only twenty cents more than your original two-dollar bet. But you could be more daring and try for the quiniela, in which you had to pick the two teams that would finish first and second but didn't have to say where they would place. Or the perfecta, in which you had to pick the first- and second-place finishers in that sequence. Or, most glorious, the trifecta, in which the three top-finishing teams had to be predicted in order. Roberto had won the trifecta once and had walked away from the cashier's window richer by $1700.

Papi would never tell anyone which teams he was putting his money on. He professed fear that the others would then bet as he had and, by increasing the odds in favor of his choice, decrease his payoff in case of victory (maybe by a thousandth of a penny, Joey would say). Mami picked teams by lucky number, betting consistently on team number four one night, nine another, while Luisa bet on a team if she liked the name of either of the players. Joey and Tom tried to bet more rationally, after glancing at the individual players' records, which they found printed in the program.

"It just stands to reason," Joey argued, "that you're going to win more if you bet a little bit intelligently. I mean, there's skill to this game; it's not like flipping coins or turning over playing cards."

But on the next game he lost two dollars and Luisa won three and a half.

"I knew that someone named Egurbi would have to win," she explained.

Roberto wasn't having a good night, though. He shrugged off the first few unsuccessful bets, saying with a laugh, "This means I'm due to win big on the next one." But he grew more and more preoccupied and irritable as the evening wore on. Like Papi, he was secretive about his betting, and never told anyone which team he was backing or how much he was betting. But Joey had been right behind him at the betting window before the last game, and he had overheard the amount of Roberto's wager, on team 7. He whispered it to Luisa and Tom, who gave a low whistle. It had been two hundred dollars. Team 3 won a narrow victory over team 7 that time, and Luisa saw Roberto's knuckles go white as he gripped the edge of his seat. Anna asked him something in a voice they couldn't hear. He turned to her and swore violently, and she didn't say anything else.

They stayed until the twelfth game, the very last one. Luisa had ended up winning her record high of seven dollars, and Tom had won six, but she kept wishing that they had lost and Roberto had won instead. She certainly wouldn't want to trade places with Anna.

"What you say we stop off for some Big Macs?" Papi asked everyone in English, as they trickled slowly back to the parking lot.

"Sorry," Roberto said, "but it'll be time to catch the seven o'clock train to New York before I know it."

"Well, good night, then," Papi said.

Joey, Tom, and Luisa climbed into the reupholstery

van with Mami and Papi, relieved that they wouldn't be riding this time with Roberto, now that the Jewishness prayer had been left unanswered.

On the way home Joey spoke to Papi for the first time since the fight about Victor's.

"Roberto lost two hundred dollars on one game alone, Papi," he said.

"So? So what am I supposed to do about it?" Papi snapped, but Luisa could tell that Papi was worried.

"Though I guess a two-hundred-dollar loss doesn't matter much when you have ten thousand dollars' worth of winnings," Joey offered, by means of adding a cheerful note.

Papi laughed harshly. "You believe that?" he asked. "You think there are ten thousand dollars in Roberto's mattress?"

Luisa felt suddenly frightened. Of course Roberto had won thousands and thousands of dollars at jai alai. So he had lost tonight. He won almost all the rest of the time.

"Roberto'll be all right," she said staunchly. "He knows what he's doing."

Tom was riding next to her on the ratty old sofa. He took her hand and gave it a reassuring squeeze. Holding fast to his, she squeezed back.

CHAPTER

9

Thursday night at exactly eight o'clock Luisa announced casually, "I've got to call Mary Beth about the algebra assignment." After dialing Travis's number, which she knew by heart, she disappeared into the bathroom, praying that his mother wouldn't answer.

"Hello," a man said, not him. His father?

"Hello," Luisa said, in an unnaturally deep voice she thought would effectively disguise her identity—not that Travis's father knew her from the man in the moon. "May I please speak to Travis?"

"Just a minute," Mr. Blaine said, and she heard him call, "Travis! Travis!"

Then: "Hello?"

Luisa took a deep breath. "Hi, Travis, this is Luisa, the girl from the dance."

" 'The girl from the dance,' " he mimicked, and Luisa knew that everything would be okay. "As if you had to tell me that. So what took you so long? I made a special point of answering the phone Monday and Tuesday so you wouldn't have to deal with my parents, but by Wednesday I decided to let you brave Mama and Papa Bear all by yourself. That is, *if* you called."

"You knew I'd call, didn't you?"

"I figured you would. So what's up?"

"Nothing, I guess."

"How's school? You said you go to Weston High?"

Luisa thought about saying yes, but he probably knew a lot of the kids there. She would have to tell him the truth—not that it was so terrible. Karen's parents sent their daughter to Our Lady of the Mountains, and they had plenty of money and weren't even Catholic. "No," she said. "Guess again."

"The Partridge School?"

"I don't know if you're getting warmer or colder: Our Lady of the Mountains."

"You're kidding!" he exclaimed. "Uniforms?"

"Uniforms."

"Little statues of the Virgin Mary all over the place?"

"You've got it."

"How do you stand it with all those frustrated nuns saying their Hail Jesuses all around you?"

"It's okay." Somehow she didn't like it when other people made fun of Our Lady, even though she did it herself, morning, noon, and night. She didn't think the nuns minded not being married and never having sex: They were married to God. And the prayer was Hail Mary, not Hail Jesus.

"So, Luisa." Her own name sounded so special when he said it. "What are you doing Saturday night?"

"Nothing, really," she said.

"How about a movie?"

"Sure."

"Anything special you want to see?"

"No," she answered. Are you kidding? she thought. It's *you* I want to see.

"Well, I'll see what's playing. I take it you still don't want me dropping by your place?"

"Right. I can meet you someplace, if that's all right. Like the Trumbull shopping center or something."

"How about seven-thirty, then. I'll look for you there, and then you can feed peeled grapes and stuff to the conquering hero for a while, before we head over to the movies. The game this weekend is at Easton, away. Any chance you might be able to catch it?"

"I'll try," Luisa promised hollowly. She'd be lucky enough to meet him Saturday night in Trumbull.

"You know, I just realized something."

"What?"

"I don't even know your last name. Luisa who?"

Luisa Williams, Luisa Adams, Luisa Miller. Luisa quickly reviewed a tentative list of more desirable names she could call herself.

"Luisa Ruiz," she said.

"Sounds Spanish. Puerto Rican?"

"Cuban."

"Of course, you're not going to find any PRs in Weston. Now that I think of it, there are a couple of Cuban families at the country club, rich as anything, and capitalist with a capital C. The day Castro took over they took their millions and split. They were in sugar, I think, had some big plantation or something. Did your folks make their money in sugar?"

"Yes," Luisa said, thinking of Papi and Abuelo coming home from the refinery in their sweat-soaked undershirts. "But it wasn't like that. I mean, not all Cubans are rich."

"Just the ones who got out."

"No, all kinds of people left. A lot just wanted to come to the United States because they thought they could do better here. You know, they heard that in the United States they could work on the assembly line today and be vice president of the company tomorrow." Had they been in for a surprise, Luisa thought, remembering Papi and Roberto's failed restaurant venture, and thinking about their situation today.

"Well, enough of the history lesson, I guess," Travis

said. "I'll see you Saturday. Oh, and one more thing."

"What is it?"

"This time, leave your brother at home."

Luisa couldn't bear the thought of being with anyone after talking to Travis. She gently hung up the receiver and quietly stole out of the bathroom to hide in her darkened bedroom, hugging the ancient stuffed rabbit. "He likes me, he likes me," she chanted. She didn't want to talk about it with Mary Beth, Karen, Tom, or anyone. "He likes me, he likes me!"

She wondered if she should regret having told Travis she was Cuban. There were certainly worse things to be: Puerto Rican, for one. There was hardly anything she minded more than having someone assume she was Puerto Rican, as Travis had done, just because she spoke Spanish. Mami and Papi had no use at all for Puerto Ricans. They thought Puerto Ricans gave all Hispanics a bad name, with their big families on welfare, their higher crime rate, and their demands for bilingual everything. "Why they no learn English?" Papi would say. Of course, the Puerto Ricans probably thought the same things about Cubans.

Luisa wondered if she would mind being Cuban if she were really the kind of Cuban Travis thought she was—a sugar heiress who had "taken her millions and split." Or even if Papi and Roberto had finally made their fortunes in their restaurant, the way her uncle Miguel had in his. A Weston Cuban would be an altogether different thing from an East Side Cuban, she had to admit. But, no, it wasn't only money she wanted; it was a whole different heritage. She wanted to be plain old American, with parents, grandparents, and great-grandparents who all spoke English. But, anyway, Travis still wanted to go out with her even after she had told him. That was the important thing.

She slipped into her parents' bedroom and took the album of their wedding pictures from the little shelf by their bed, below the statue of the Blessed Virgin Mary. That was like Mami: They had left Cuba with one small suitcase for the four of them, but in it Mami had made room for her wedding pictures. Luisa knew she would have done the same. She flipped slowly through the pages of familiar pictures. Mami and Papi both looked so young; Mami had been a girl of eighteen and Papi hardly any older. Mami's beautiful white wedding dress with all its loving, laborious handwork was carefully packed away in Teresa's house, waiting for Luisa if she ever went back to Cuba. But she knew she never would, not to stay. Even Mami and Papi wouldn't now, not even if Castro were to be sent into exile tomorrow. They were American citizens. Not Americans the way that Mary Beth, Karen, and Travis were, but Americans all the same.

"Oh, Travis," Luisa thought, putting the wedding album away, "I hope you know that. I want so much for you to like me."

CHAPTER

10

Luisa was not good for very much in school on Friday. Sister Angela, her favorite nun, even called her up to the front desk after class to ask why the star history student had gotten fourteen wrong on the test. Luisa wanted to tell her, but she wasn't sure nuns approved of dating, or of boys. Sister Marguerita didn't seem to. Luisa remembered guiltily Travis's hand under her sweater.

She decided to go ahead and tell her. "I'm in love, Sister," she confessed, and Sister Angela just beamed.

"Is he a Catholic?" she asked fondly.

"No," Luisa said. "But I think he's a Protestant."

"Oh," Sister Angela said, and stopped beaming.

At lunchtime, the girls talked about nothing but Travis.

"You don't mean Travis *Blaine,* do you?" Karen asked suddenly.

"Do you know him?" Luisa asked, and desperately wondered: What if Travis were dating Karen, too? What if he had even joked to her about this crazy kid who had such a crush on him? Or if he had kissed Karen in the front seat of the blue Mustang, just as he had kissed her?

"Not really." Luisa's heart started beating again. "My parents know his parents, and I met him at a party, last summer I think it was, at the country club."

"And?" Luisa and Mary Beth demanded.

"And nothing. I'm surprised I didn't make the connection before this—there can't be that many Travises in Trumbull. It's just that—somehow I didn't think that—"

"That a guy like Travis would look twice at somebody like me. Go ahead and say it."

"No, not that at all—you didn't let me finish. What I was trying to say was—it's more—well, the opposite. It's not that I really know him, or anything, but from what I know, he isn't anybody you should be losing any sleep over."

"Are you sure we're talking about the same person?"

"Travis Blaine. He's very good-looking. And good at sports. I remember we played some volleyball, he and I and a bunch of kids, and he was the best player on our side. But there are good-looking jocks all over the place, so if that's all he is—though I could be wrong about him, Luisa, and maybe I shouldn't even be telling you any of this. I'm no big expert on character or anything."

Well, Karen *was* wrong about Travis—there was no question about that.

"Did he flirt with all the girls at the party?" she asked. After all, it was better that she should know.

"Nooo," Karen said slowly. "Not exactly flirt. But he knows he's very attractive and that he can pretty much go out with any girl he wants."

"Well, that's true," Luisa defended him. "He's just recognizing a fact."

"Maybe," Karen said.

"So what should she wear tomorrow night?" Mary Beth asked then, starting in with her little wooden spoon on the chocolate half of her Dixie cup. "It's time to get practical, girls."

Luisa looked inquiringly at Karen.

"I'd say your denim skirt." Karen leaned back in her chair and cocked her head to the side, the better to envision Luisa in the outfit. "And that blouse you got when we went shopping the last time, the scoop-necked peasant one. You look good in ivory."

"Casual, but feminine," Mary Beth pronounced. "But now, how are you going to get out of the house and over to Trumbull by seven-thirty?"

"I can get out of the house by saying I'm going to watch TV with you. But getting to Trumbull by seven-thirty . . . I don't suppose I could ride my bike?" Luisa said. "No. Can't you see Travis trying to stick it in the back of the Mustang!"

"Would your brother be able to drive you?" Karen asked.

"He might break down and drive me to the mall again, but that still leaves getting home. Unless—unless Joey'd come pick me up later on if I called him. But, no, he's covered for me enough already. And I can't see him spending his Saturday night driving me places, especially places he doesn't approve of. I don't think he's wild about Travis."

"What makes you think that?" Karen asked.

"I don't know, really. It's nothing he's said. It's more what he hasn't said. It's funny, Tom's acting a lot more like a big brother than Joey is, really concerned and protective, you know, almost jealous. There's just this funny way his voice gets when he asks me about my 'Trumbull Romeo.' "

"Tom," Mary Beth said. "How about Tom? Make Joey drive you to the mall—you can tell your parents you're coming over to my house. That'll be good since my parents will be out for the evening and I can think of something if your mom calls you up there. And then have Travis drop you off at Victor's when Tom gets off from work, probably pretty late on a Saturday."

It sounded like another one of Mary Beth's genius plans, but Luisa was still doubtful. "Do you think Travis would mind? I mean, dropping his date off to see another guy?"

"No, just say Tom's your cousin. Look, Travis'll know that if Tom were a real romantic possibility, you wouldn't let him find out on your first date."

"Don't you think Tom might mind?" Karen asked.

"Of course not. I'm sure he's on my side against Mami and Papi. What could he possibly mind about?"

"You figure it out," Karen said. "I have to go factor six more quadratic equations between now and sixth period."

Joey and Tom were finally both pressed into service, according to Mary Beth's arrangement. And Tom seemed perfectly willing to give Luisa a ride home from Victor's—which proved that Karen didn't know everything.

"Sure," he said, when she approached him about it that evening. "And I'll even throw in some free pizza—how's that for a deal you won't be able to top?"

"You're sure that you're sure?"

"Anything for a kid sister of my old St. Charles schoolyard war buddy."

Joey, however, was not so easily persuaded into doing his part.

"Why doesn't this guy—Travis, or whatever his name is—pick you up and take you home? If you think Mami and Papi wouldn't like your dating anyone yet—and they sure as heck wouldn't—he could just honk the horn for you, and then quietly drop you off afterward. He wouldn't have to come in and eat two pieces of pie with Mami and rehash the whole World Series with Papi or anything. Listen, when I go out with a girl I don't expect her to provide her own transportation to and from the street corner where it's most convenient for me to pick her up."

"It's my idea to meet him there, not his."

"It's a lousy idea, whosever it is."

"Well, why don't you just invite your next date to join you for cocktails at the Good Times bar, then? Why don't you just tell her you happen to know this charming little place where you can go for a romantic drink before dinner?"

"I don't see what that has to do with any of this."

"Why don't you just walk around with a T-shirt that says 'I love the East Side'?"

"If you got one printed up for me, I'd wear it," Joey said, but then he stopped joking. "I'm getting pretty sick of your grand too-good-for-Bridgeport airs."

"You don't have to be all that grand to be too good for Bridgeport," Luisa shot back.

"How about too good for your family?"

"If you don't want to drive me to Trumbull, just say so. There are plenty of ways I can get there without your driving me. I can hitchhike—"

"Oh, give me a break. That's not even funny. You know I'll drive you to see your super-snob, super-WASP date. But for the record, I think it's lousy to be ashamed of your family. And I think your Travis is a creep to meet you on the street corner, whatever kind of line you've used on him."

"Anything else, Mr. Perfect?" Luisa asked, furious to find herself fighting back tears.

"Be ready right at seven, 'cause I'm not going to wait."

But Luisa refused to let herself feel guilty: Everything was all set for her first date with Travis! She crossed off the hours until one-thirty Saturday afternoon, when

there were only six hours left, and then she started cross-
ing off the half hours; at four-thirty, the quarter hours,
and then, as she brushed and brushed her freshly sham-
pooed hair and applied just a little bit of eyeshadow and
mascara, the minutes. By seven she was almost dancing
with happy excitement.

Even Joey acknowledged that she looked pretty.
"Going out with creeps seems to agree with you," he told
her. He dropped her off at the mall at seven-fifteen—it
wouldn't do to be a minute late for her first date with
Travis!—and she walked around the entire mall seven
times, anxiously catching her reflection in all the store
windows. Her hair looked just right, dark against the
ivory of the blouse, though maybe the skirt was a little
too short? And the less said about her jacket, the better.
She practiced smiling, and the girl mirrored in the windows smiled back at her, radiantly in love.

But then it was seven forty-five, and Travis still hadn't
arrived. Suddenly she knew, as certainly as she had ever
known anything, that he wasn't going to come. He wasn't
going to come. Oddly, she didn't feel heartbroken or angry, just perfectly numb. She wondered fleetingly how
she would get home. She could call Tom at Victor's, and
he would come to pick her up after work, but how was
she going to get through the hours and hours between
the time the mall would close and whenever the last Victor's pizza would be delivered? Tears stung her eyes
now—it seemed that ever since he had shouted at her as
she lay sprawled on the dirty pavement, she had felt close
to tears. But now the romance was over, and that was
better, really. Or it would be—after a while.

She turned to go, and he was there.

CHAPTER

11

"How about *Invasion of the Killer Reptiles?*" he asked. Either he didn't notice that she had been crying, or he was too polite to mention it. "It's at eight, so we've got to hurry."

She had never loved him like this. No one had ever loved anyone like this.

"Psst," he hissed at her, taking her hand and leaning toward her, as if he were about to reveal an important secret. "You look great."

The movie, Luisa admitted, wasn't great at all, but it was terrific to sit with Travis in the darkened theater, side by side, on a date. She had been so excited about her first date with Travis that she had forgotten it was her very first date.

She had brought enough money to pay for her own movie ticket, and felt that she ought to walk right up to the lady in the ticket booth and boldly say, "One, please." She was liberated enough not to expect some guy to have to pay her way. But he had taken it for granted that he was paying, and had bought her popcorn as well, with wonderful, greasy, two-thousand-calories-to-a-mouthful butter dripping all over it. She was going to eat only a little bit, but after he had finished his, he started in on hers, and fed her a few handfuls.

Luisa had hoped the movie would be real scary, so that she could bury her face in the Trumbull sweater and have Travis hold her close to him. But try as she would, she couldn't get scared. The movie was just too stupid. Travis didn't seem to need an excuse to hold her, anyway. As soon as the opening credits appeared on the screen he began squeezing her neck and shoulder, and as

81

the final reptile slithered into the quicksand, he kissed her.

"I'm starved," he said when it was over. "You must be, too. You hardly ate any popcorn at all."

They drove to the Golden Dream diner and headed for a booth in the back. Luisa opened the menu and read the description of the cheese blintzes, even though she knew all she was going to have was a Tab.

A white-jacketed guy with reddish hair and freckles came around with a pad to take their orders. Travis ordered a Coke and a cheeseburger platter with french fries and coleslaw.

"Is it okay if I have just a Tab?" Luisa asked the waiter, who looked like the kind who wouldn't mind.

"Well, they usually have a dollar minimum at booths, but for you, the requirement is waived."

He smiled, and suddenly Luisa knew where she had seen him before.

"Aren't you Luisa?" he asked then.

"Doug."

"Right. How's Mary Beth?"

"She's okay." She wanted to add, "She'd be even more okay if you called her," but Travis was there. Besides, she wasn't sure Mary Beth would appreciate that kind of assistance.

"Tell her hi for me, will you?"

"Okay."

"Don't forget, now," he said when he returned a minute later with their drinks.

Travis eyed her Tab suspiciously. "Are you one of those girls who are on a diet all the time?"

"No," Luisa lied. "I'm just not hungry tonight."

Then Doug brought the food, and they sat in silence.

Luisa wished it were easier to talk to Travis. But it seemed that anything she would talk about would be something she didn't want him to know about in the first place. Her family. Joey and the job at Victor's. Roberto and jai alai. Our Lady of the Mountains. Well, he already knew that she went to a Catholic girls' school, so maybe school would be a safe subject. She tried to remember things she had read in the advice columns in the newspaper. Get him to talk about himself, they had said.

"Are you a senior?" she asked.

"You better believe it. How about you?"

"Sophomore."

She waited and took another sip of Tab.

"Are you getting ready to apply to college for next year?"

"Yeah, and it is the royal pain of the century. My father wants me to apply to Amherst, Wesleyan, Dartmouth, places like that. My grades pretty much stink, but I guess my folks think they'll take me on good looks and charm. And because my father went to Amherst and my uncles went to the others. But even if I got in, which would be an A-one miracle, I don't feel like busting ass for four years just to get by."

Dartmouth! The Ivy League! Just the thought of visiting Travis up there on a big football weekend made Luisa's pulse race.

"Where do you want to go?" she asked.

"U. Conn., I guess. I know a lot of guys there and they have an all right time. I buy some weed off them now and then. Do you smoke?"

"You mean, smoke marijuana?" As soon as she'd asked, Luisa realized how dumb the question sounded.

"Yeah, get high."

"No, I never have. But it's not that I have anything against it. My brother smokes sometimes. I guess I just never got around to it."

"Would you like to? I've got some stuff with me."

"Sure," Luisa said, with automatic enthusiasm, exactly the way she would have responded had he asked, "Would you like to fly to the moon?" But she felt a little bit scared. She had never even smoked cigarettes, except once with Mary Beth and Karen. It had been terrible: She remembered choking on the smoke and feeling dizzy and nauseous whenever she managed to inhale properly. But she would smoke marijuana with Travis if it killed her. Papi believed you could become addicted after smoking it once, and said he had never heard of anyone who had smoked grass without later becoming hooked on heroin. But Joey and Tom both smoked, so it had to be okay.

They drove over to Seaside Park. There was no moon, and the waters of the Sound were perfectly black. A few stars twinkled. Luisa made a quick wish on the first one she saw: Let him keep on liking me.

Travis parked the car and, leaning over Luisa, opened the glove compartment. He took out a little Baggie with what looked like crumbled brown autumn leaves. She had seen little bags like that in Joey's underwear drawer. But her brother used a little wooden pipe, while Travis proceeded to roll up his own marijuana cigarettes. Expertly, he licked the rolling papers to seal each one. Then he struck a match and took a deep drag on the first joint. He didn't speak for a couple of minutes afterward, holding the smoke in his lungs for as long as possible. He handed the cigarette to Luisa.

Here goes, she thought, and tried to take in the smoke as she had seen Travis do. It was hot and bitter, worse even than the Kools she'd tried. She compressed her lips tightly after the first puff, but she felt that the smoke hadn't really entered her lungs. It was just trapped in her mouth and throat. Travis exhaled a big cloud of smoke, but when Luisa released her breath, nothing came out.

"Did you get a good hit?" he asked, and Luisa nodded, beginning to feel rather miserable.

She did her best through the whole cigarette, although she felt afraid of burning her fingers toward the end. When the joint got too small to hold, Luisa felt relieved that finally the hateful object would be tossed out the window, joining the cigarette butts littering the sand. But Travis, with a slow smile, produced a pair of tweezers, and, holding the joint end between the two prongs, continued dragging away.

"How do you feel?" he murmured, pulling her close to him across the console.

Luisa wasn't about to tell him she didn't feel anything except a dry and acrid taste in her mouth. She tried smiling what she imagined to be a stoned person's smile—a little bit dazed, a little bit silly.

"I know," he said. "Isn't it crazy when you find yourself just *smiling?*"

He kissed her, and this time she was ready for his groping tongue. She didn't feel quite so much as if she were choking to death.

"Ummmm," he sighed, when she finally struggled away from him to come up for breath. "Smoking always makes it better."

They kissed some more. Travis squeezed her shoulders and began slowly to massage her back. He slipped his hand around to the front of her blouse, and, through the thin cloth of her blouse, rubbed against her breast. She wanted to tell him not to, as she had at the dance, but suddenly it did seem rather stupid, whatever Mary Beth might say, that he could touch her back and side, but not a certain portion of her front. But why did she feel so different when he touched that part of it? She reached her arms around him, and thrilled as her hands roamed his muscular back.

He lit up another joint, and, after they had smoked it down to the tiny bit held in the tweezers, they made out some more. This time she let his hands move under her blouse. He deftly unhooked her bra, even though it was the untraditional kind that fastened in the front, and Luisa wondered how many girls he had parked with before, and if he had been with another girl even last night.

"I have to go soon," she whispered.

"I want you so much, Luisa," he said, and she felt his hands tighten on her.

"I love you, Travis," she said. "I love you."

Suddenly, she heard a church clock somewhere strike once. She waited for the other eleven peals to follow, but they didn't.

"It isn't one o'clock, is it?" she asked, tugging at her blouse and pushing her tangled hair back from her face.

"It sure is."

"But I have to go. I told Tom I'd be there by twelve."

"Is Tom your brother?"

"No, he's my brother's best friend. He works at Victor's Pizzeria and he said he'd drop me off at home if I got there before they closed."

"They're still open, I think, and, anyway, I can always give you a ride. It's not a bad drive to Weston."

But I don't live in Weston, Luisa thought frantically.

"Oh, but my parents'll be spying out the window," she

said, "to see who's driving the car I come home in."

All the way to Victor's she prayed for Tom to be there. Thank goodness Travis was a fast driver and not too scrupulous about stopping at every red light. As they approached Victor's, Luisa saw Tom's familiar old Chevy in front of the darkened pizza parlor.

"That his car?" Travis asked.

It did look ready for the junkyard, but Luisa didn't care that Travis had seen what sort of hot rod her friends drove around in. She was just so relieved.

"One last kiss," Travis ordered, and his mouth bore down on hers. But Luisa felt uncomfortable kissing him, with Tom parked right there across the street, and she pulled her lips away.

"Call me?" he said.

"I will," she promised hastily, and ran to where Tom was waiting.

CHAPTER

12

"I didn't think you'd still be here," Luisa apologized.

"Then you don't know me very well," Tom said, starting the engine.

"Were you waiting long?"

"Not too long. Forty-five minutes, maybe. What are your parents going to say when you waltz in at a quarter to two? They must have called Mary Beth's house half a dozen times to find out why you weren't home yet."

Luisa hadn't even let herself think about Mami and Papi and how they'd be waiting for her. Papi had probably called the police and the Mother Superior. Perhaps at this very moment all the sisters from Our Lady of the Mountains were out combing the streets, searching every dark alleyway, saying rosaries on her behalf. No. It wasn't funny.

"Maybe they didn't wait up," she suggested. After all, they had thought she was at Mary Beth's. No need for any special vigils, or candles burning in the windows.

"Maybe," Tom said. "And maybe the Pope's not Catholic, either."

But what could they do to her, really? Luisa asked herself. Papi could hit her, but he hadn't done that for years. The last time he had taken off his belt to punish her, he had practically broken it right across her backside, furious because she had refused to cry. She and Joey had driven him to distraction when they were little, because Joey always cried and Luisa never did. Hot tears welled up in her eyes now.

Maybe Papi would never let her go out again, or at least not for months and months. Then she wouldn't see

Travis anymore. He would forget her in time and begin to flirt with some of the girls from the country club. Maybe he wouldn't even miss her. She turned away from Tom's glance and stared out the window, clenching her teeth to keep herself under control. They passed the Good Times bar—two men dressed up as women were loitering outside, with their arms around each other's waist—and then turned the corner onto Luisa's street.

Tom had been right: The lights were on at 446 Tilden Street, and Luisa could hear her parents' raised voices before she even left the car.

"Do you want me to come in with you?" Tom asked.

"No," Luisa said, "I'd better go in alone."

Mami hugged her and cried and called Abuela to tell her that Luisa was safe and sound, that no one had hurt her, and she had come home. Papi shouted and started to unbuckle his belt, calling her a whore and a slut, a disgrace to her family and to her father's name. Joey looked at her with cold disapproval, as if he didn't know her. He must have received his share of shouting when he came home at midnight to find that Papi had already called Mary Beth's. Through it all she felt oddly detached, as though it were all happening to someone else and she were just an observer, watching this bizarre family drama. She heard her own voice saying, "I don't see why you're all so upset. I didn't do anything so terrible," and was surprised at how sure and confident she sounded.

"No nice girl lies to her parents and stays out until two o'clock with a man they don't even know!" Papi shouted, gesturing with his belt, which he now clenched doubled-over in his hand. "No nice girl worries her Mami and whores around with some bum!"

"I'm sorry if you and Mami were worried," Luisa said,

and when she saw tears streaming down Mami's cheeks she was sorrier still.

"You aren't sorry that you stayed out half the night with your—boyfriend?" Papi spat out the last word as if it were a curse.

"Joey stays out late all the time," Luisa argued. "And he stayed out late when he was a sophomore, too."

"José has nothing to do with it!" Papi cracked his belt violently against the old sofa. "The two situations have nothing at all in common!"

"Why not?" Luisa asked. She didn't have anything more to lose. "Just because Joey's a boy?"

Papi swore and stomped out of the room, only to storm back in a moment later. "Give me the phone," he ordered. "I'm going to call your Sister Bernice at that school where I pay good money to send you and ask her what they are teaching little girls nowadays."

Mami caught Papi's arm. "Ernesto, no, it is so late. The sisters are all asleep."

"That's right, and the parents are all awake, because their daughters don't respect their families and come home at three o'clock in the morning! What is this boy's name, Luisa? Maybe I should call him up so that he and I can have a little talk, yes? He's still up, I'm sure. His kind don't get much sleep."

Luisa didn't answer his question. She was glad even Joey didn't know Travis's last name.

"It isn't fair to treat Joey differently," she persisted.

"Don't you question your Papi!" he shouted. He grabbed Luisa's arm, pulled her over to him, and raised his belt. Luisa set her mouth stubbornly, waiting for the blows. But they didn't come. The belt hung limply from Papi's hand.

"I don't know why anyone has children," he said, and

he sounded as close to weeping as Luisa had ever heard him. "You would give your life for them, and they don't even love or respect you. They want to go to work for strangers. They disgrace your good name. José, Luisa, do what you want, both of you. I'm not going to fight you anymore. Go deliver your pizzas. I'll pay someone to help me in the shop. Stay out all night with your boyfriends. But when you have your bastard babies, don't come to me with your problems. I've had enough."

He turned away and walked heavily off to bed.

"Nice job, Luisa," Joey said disgustedly, breaking the silence that followed Papi's departure.

"No, José," Mami said. "Leave your sister alone. She feels bad enough already. Why don't you go to bed now, too, and Luisa and I will talk, just we two women all by ourselves."

Joey gave Mami a good-night kiss, which he hardly ever did anymore, and, without giving Luisa another look, disappeared into his room.

"You don't have to be so nice about it," Luisa began with difficulty, once they were alone. Mami's standing up for her made her feel even more like crying than Papi's parting speech had.

"I remember in Cuba," Mami said, gently pulling Luisa's head into her lap and twisting her hair idly into braids as she talked, "one time when I was still a young girl, before I had met your Papi—I sneaked out of my room at night when Abuelo and Abuela were asleep to meet a man."

Luisa tried to turn her head to look at Mami in surprise, but Mami's fingers kept on plaiting.

"Not even Consuela ever knew, and, of course, not your Papi."

"What happened?"

"We just went for a walk, by the ocean. He didn't even hold my hand. But I felt so guilty afterward that I would never speak to him again, and afraid, too. Because if anyone had seen me with him and spread stories that Maria went walking alone with strange men, then, whatever the truth of the matter was, no one would have listened to me. In their minds, I would have been a whore, like the girls who walked the streets in Havana, and not a nice girl anymore. People would even have whispered about Consuela, just because of what I, her sister, had done."

It was good to feel Mami's fingers making the braids and to hear Mami talk, her voice low and soothing now so as not to wake Joey or Papi.

"You know why Papi is so angry, don't you, baby?"

"I guess so."

"He only wants what's best for you and José. That's why he works so hard, so that you two can go to college and be college graduates and have nice jobs someday. And he wants the best for you in every way. We want you to marry a nice man, a man like your father or your brother. Now, I have eyes and I can see how things are different here from how they were when I was a girl like you in my country. I think in some ways it's good, too. I don't want you to feel guilty about just being with a boy. But I do want you to make sure you know what you're doing, and not to do anything you don't think is right. And I don't want you to lie to your Mami and Papi."

"I know, Mami, and I'm sorry, I really am." Luisa tried to open her eyes just a crack, but her eyelids felt so heavy, as if tiny invisible weights were resting on them.

"You're sleepy, that's what you are," Mami said then, helping her to sit up and giving her face a kiss. "Off to bed with you now. And tomorrow everything'll be all right with your Papi. You'll see."

CHAPTER

13

When Luisa woke up the next morning, Papi had already taken the van and left for the day, without telling Mami where he was going or when he would be back. Luisa heard the van back out of the driveway, and pulled up the coverlet she had kicked off during her restless sleep. She punched the lumpy pillow into shape and lay there thinking. Mami had said everything would be better today, but Luisa was pretty sure nothing had changed.

Had Papi meant what he said about Joey's job at Victor's and her dating Travis? Did he still love both of them after everything that had happened? She wished she could tell him she wouldn't see Travis again, that next weekend she would truly go to Mary Beth's and cut pictures of Robert Redford out of magazines the way they used to. Or at least that she wouldn't go out with anyone she couldn't bring home to meet her family. In all fairness, she knew that was all they would ask of her, and it didn't seem unreasonable. Or it wouldn't have—if she had had a different kind of family. She didn't even want them to be all that different: Mary Beth's or Karen's mother couldn't be any more understanding than Mami had been.

She looked at the clock. It was too late for mass. Without bothering to comb out the braids Mami had woven, she tiptoed through Joey's half of the room into the kitchen. Mami hadn't gone to church, either; she was sitting alone at the kitchen table in her enormous terry-cloth cocoon, eating oven-toasted chunks of stale Spanish bread with butter and guava jelly.

Luisa hesitantly joined her at the table.

"Where did Papi go?"

Mami shrugged. She sliced bread to toast for Luisa and poured her a cup of *café con leche,* coffee strongly diluted with sweet, thick, condensed milk.

"What I don't understand," Mami said, without preamble, "is why this boy doesn't come to our house to visit you. We told you we didn't want you dating any boys yet. But that doesn't mean he couldn't come over and watch the ball game with your father, and maybe even come with us all to the movies or jai alai. That way you could see each other, but your Papi and I wouldn't have to worry."

Luisa cupped her hands around the steaming mug.

"I couldn't get to sleep last night wondering about it, but now I think—I think I understand. Are you ashamed of this boy?" Mami asked gently. "Is he someone you think your Papi and I wouldn't approve of?"

Luisa looked out the back window and saw the long line of Papi's undershirts and shorts flapping in the raw, gray morning breeze across the rusty fire escape. The Spanish Sunday paper littered the floor, and the radio blared lively Latin music. Mami was eating her fourteenth piece of toast and jam, guava jam, dunked in Spanish coffee.

"I guess so," she said with some effort.

Joey came into the kitchen barefoot, his shirt unbuttoned, rubbing sleep from his eyes.

"Do you want some eggs, José?" Mami offered. "I have sausage and bacon, too."

He grunted, which Mami took for an enthusiastic affirmative. In an instant three eggs were prepared for scrambling, the bacon was sizzling in the pan, and several chunks of hot, toasted bread had been generously buttered and set before him.

In between rumbas the Spanish disc jockey bellowed that the weather would continue cloudy and unseasonably cold until the middle of the week. Mami deftly turned the bacon and eggs onto Joey's plate and gave herself a shivering hug.

"Do you remember, José, Luisa," she asked, "how sunny and warm it was every day in Cuba? And, José, I remember we told you children there would be snow in the United States, and as soon as we got to Miami you asked, 'Where's the snow?' In Miami, you asked this!"

"I have something to say, Mami," Joey said then, before Mami could go off on one of her orgies of reminiscing. "I'm going to take Papi at his word. I'm going to tell Tom I want the job at Victor's."

"You will break his heart," Mami said, her smile abruptly disappearing.

"He'll get over it," Joey said, with greater callousness than he felt. "He knows I'll still go on deliveries with him. He just wants to keep me under his thumb forever."

The whole day was miserable. Papi didn't come home. Joey drove over to Victor's with Tom—Victor always needed extra help on weekends. Mami ate the better part of the canned ham she had been saving for Sunday dinner. And Luisa locked herself in the bathroom for a session on the phone with Mary Beth.

"Guess who works in the Golden Dream?" she asked right away.

"I don't know. The guy from the Laundromat?"

"No." She paused for effect. "Doug. Doug from the dance."

"Oh. That's nice," Mary Beth said.

"Is that all you have to say about it?" Luisa asked. " 'That's nice'? He said to say hello to you. He said it twice. He said I should be sure not to forget."

There was silence on the other end of the line.

"I think he likes you, Mary Beth. I really do."

"You worry about me too much," Mary Beth said finally. "When I'm meant to have a boyfriend I'll have one. You can't rush these things. There's even a song like that: 'You Can't Hurry Love.' "

"But there's waiting and then there's waiting—"

"And speaking of waiting, do you realize that I've been sitting by the phone since eight o'clock this morning dying to hear the Trumbull date report?"

Luisa made herself comfortable on the shaggy throw rug, with her back against the tub, and launched into a blow by blow recounting of the first date. Then she and Mary Beth planned strategies for appeasing Mami and Papi while keeping Travis interested.

If she had been talking to Karen instead—and she was glad Karen was away at her grandparents', so she wouldn't have to tell her the latest news until she had sorted it out herself—Karen would have asked her why she wanted to keep Travis interested in the first place. Mary Beth, of course, knew perfectly well without asking. And Luisa knew. She could list reasons she loved Travis just as easily as she could list reasons she hated so much else. His curly *blond* hair. His uncanny resemblance to a younger Robert Redford. The casual, relaxed, even careless way he drove, with his strong hands resting so lightly on the steering wheel. His incredible self-assurance— Travis didn't have anything to be apologetic about. She even liked the way he wanted to feel her up when they were parking in the Mustang, although it frightened her, too. But at least he wasn't a *prude*, the way some of those St. Francis of Assisi guys were. The stuff in the car just showed he was normal, instead of Catholic. And he needed her, too, in a way, really he did. Because Travis didn't seem to care about anything—he didn't even seem excited when he talked about football. It was almost as if he talked about it because that was what guys on the team were supposed to talk about. Luisa, on the other hand, had had plenty of experience in wanting and needing and missing things. She would teach him how to care.

Mary Beth listened as patiently as ever, but as soon as the conversation was over Luisa realized the person she had really wanted to talk to was Travis himself. But she didn't want to call him so soon after seeing him, and she certainly didn't want to cry on his shoulder. Or was that exactly what she wanted to do? It seemed like an eternity ago that she had led the campaign against Sister Bernice on the makeup issue and put the sisters of Our Lady high on her hate list. The hate list hadn't gotten her anywhere—it wasn't the makeup, the school uniforms, the reupholstery chores, and the black beans with rice that were the problem. It was her entire life: her house, her family, herself. But, no, she couldn't tell Travis that. She dialed his number, anyway. His mother answered and she hung up. Later, when she tried again, he answered the phone himself. But she slowly replaced the receiver without speaking. She wouldn't be a pest.

Abuela and Abuelo came over later in the afternoon with Roberto, Anna, and Bobby. While Abuelo and Roberto watched a cable football game, Abuelo ogling the scantily clad cheerleaders, the women gathered in the shop to keep Mami company as she stitched long drapery seams on the sewing machine.

"How's the little girl across the street?" Luisa asked, figuring she deserved more punishment for her curfew violation. Anna didn't seem to want to talk any more about Bobby's romantic prowess. She looked tired, and one side of her face was redder than the other, as if she had slept on it wrong.

"Did Roberto lose last night?" Mami asked her. The directness of the question made Luisa wince.

"No," Anna said, without meeting Mami's eyes. "We didn't go." She glanced at Bobby, who was intently taking apart an Oreo sandwich cookie and licking off the cream filling in between. "Your father wants you," she said, and he went off, leaving the cookie pieces behind him on the floor.

"I'm just tired," Anna said, with a little laugh. "My headaches have come back again and I haven't been sleeping well at night."

"You need a vacation, all of you," Mami suggested. "You should make your husband take you away for a week or two, maybe down to Florida to visit Miguel."

"Vacations cost too much," Anna replied with uncharacteristic shortness. "All I need is a good night's sleep."

The phone rang. "I'll get it," Luisa called. Maybe it was Travis.

But it wasn't. It was Anna's father, Jaime, who lived downstairs from Roberto and Anna. Luisa remembered that he used to be a lot of fun, telling sea stories for hours—he had been a fisherman back in Cuba—when Anna's mother was alive. But after she had died of cancer two years ago, he had for the most part stopped talking to anyone. It was a lucky thing he had Roberto and Anna to keep an eye on him, because for a while now he had been growing more and more absentminded and forgetful. Once a whole day had gone by without his remembering to eat.

But today he was highly agitated, so excited that Luisa could hardly understand what he was saying. She stuck her finger in her other ear to block out the football game and Mami's jabbering, and forced herself to listen. He said that the house had been broken into, and he had been robbed. There had been five hundred dollars in a shoe box in the back of his closet, and it was gone, box and all. He broke down sobbing.

Luisa told him, in as calming a tone as she could manage, that Anna and Roberto would be right over, and ran to tell them the news, wishing now that Papi were home. Thank goodness, at least Roberto was there. He would know what to do. She was so relieved that she wouldn't be the only one who spoke English when the police came over, forced to answer their questions all by herself.

Anna was almost hysterical. "My silver! My silver!" she kept crying. She had left an exquisite set of solid silver tableware behind her in Cuba, since none of them had been allowed to take anything of material value when they emigrated; the women had even left their gold and diamond wedding rings in the safekeeping of relatives. Roberto had replaced that set of silver for her, piece by piece, and it was her pride and joy. She shook uncontrollably with sobs.

They all crowded into Roberto's car and quickly drove the few blocks to Jaime's.

"Damn Puerto Ricans," Abuelo swore. "Goddamn Puerto Ricans."

Anna ran upstairs while the others swarmed into Jaime's apartment. She rejoined them in a minute: The silver was still there, the Blessed Virgin be praised! She burst out crying again, this time with relief.

Downstairs everyone was talking at once, trying to

piece together exactly what had happened: what was missing, how and when it had been stolen, and who the thief or thieves might be. Abuela and Abuelo had been robbed two months ago, and had lost some cash—though not as much as Jaime—and the cable receiver from the top of the TV. Abuela had been out of the apartment fifteen minutes, twenty at most. The police said it must have been an inside job, and although nothing was ever proved, everyone suspected the Puerto Ricans two floors up. Their teen-age boys had been in trouble with the law before.

Jaime was sure the money had been there yesterday morning, because he had taken some out to buy groceries on his weekly shopping expedition with Roberto and Anna. But this afternoon, when he went to the closet he found the shoe box gone. He had left the house only twice yesterday, once to go grocery shopping and once to go to Lou's Variety Store to put some money on the Jets football game.

"Did you lock the door each time?" Roberto asked.

"Yes, I did." He put his hand to his head, as if trying to fasten his thoughts. "I think I did."

Abuelo and Roberto examined the lock. It showed no signs of having been tampered with.

"Could you have forgotten one time?" Roberto asked.

"Sure, I could have," Jaime admitted, more and more confused. "But I don't think so," he added uncertainly.

"Luisa will call the police," Mami volunteered, motioning her toward the kitchen, where the phone was.

"They won't do anything," Roberto said disgustedly. "They'll just ask Jaime how old he is so that they can publish his age in the papers. What else can they do? This is Bridgeport. Dozens of houses are broken into every week—they never find out who did it."

Mami hesitated. "But the police should at least know about it," she said. "And who knows? Maybe this time they'll find the crook."

By the time the police arrived, everyone was calmer. Anna had brought beer and soda down from upstairs and a couple of bags of potato chips. The Cuban family in crisis, Luisa thought. Bring out the food. Two policemen came, and although they were very sympathetic, Roberto had been right. They weren't at all optimistic about recovering Jaime's cash. And the first thing they did was record Jaime's age on their official case clipboard.

Roberto gave Mami and Luisa a ride home afterward. Nobody in the car felt much like talking. Luisa told herself she was glad, at least, that Mami and Papi had something to worry about besides what time she had come home from her date with Travis. But then she thought about Jaime's choked sobs over the telephone, and she knew she wasn't glad at all.

CHAPTER

14

Papi was only partly true to his word. Although he maintained a grim silence when Joey came home late every night with leftover pizza, he wasn't equally resigned to Luisa's seeing Travis. In fact, he laid down the law: no more dating until she turned fifteen, no dating at all unless the date was first introduced to him and Mami, and always home by midnight.

There was nothing Luisa could say to persuade him otherwise. She couldn't even employ her favorite strategy for appealing his decisions in such cases: telling him that the "real American" parents of her friends were all letting them do whatever was in question. Mary Beth's parents were almost as strict as Luisa's—that's what you got for having Catholic parents—and even Karen's parents, although they let her date, insisted on meeting "the young man" first. Luisa could not even imagine Travis's coming over to the house, as Tom did, trading insults with Papi and letting Mami stuff him with fried bananas. But she couldn't imagine never seeing him again, either.

"Look," Mary Beth said, as she, Karen, and Luisa sat at their favorite corner table in the lunchroom on Monday, analyzing the situation. "There are just three possibilities. You can go on disobeying your parents, clue Travis in to your—ahem—ethnic heritage and socioeconomic status, or you can forget it. Take your pick."

"Which would you pick?" Luisa asked her.

"Oh, I don't know, Lu. You're the one who has to decide."

"Karen?"

"I know what *I'd* do," she said slowly, "but I'm not sure you want to hear it."

"You'd just forget it."

"Believe me, Luisa, there are dozens of Travises at the country club, there really are. You can't climb out of the pool without tripping over one of them."

"You met Travis *once.*"

"I know, but some people you know you've seen before. Anyway, you asked what I'd do, and I told you."

"If you didn't forget it, what would you do?"

"Okay, I think you should have Travis come over to your house so you can find out exactly what he's like. I may not think he's Mr. Wonderful or anything, but he isn't a creep. I bet he'd really love your family—everyone loves your mom and dad—and he'd probably get a big kick out of hearing everyone speak Spanish and eating authentic Spanish food and everything."

"Sort of like a mini Cuban holiday right in your own backyard?" Luisa asked, spearing a ravioli savagely with her fork. "I don't think so. If people like Travis want a Spanish holiday, they fly to Spain."

"His parents aren't all that well off," Karen said. "They don't have any more money than mine." Luisa and Mary Beth exchanged a look. Karen had spent her last vacation in St. Thomas and the vacation before that in London.

"Forget it," Luisa said. "It's all decided. He's never coming to my house. Ever. And I happen to want to see him again, however many Travises you may think you know. I'm just going to make sure that this time they don't find out."

"But how are you going to have any kind of relationship if you're not honest with him?" Karen protested.

Luisa grabbed hold of her tray and stood up suddenly. "I said to forget it. What do you know about this, Karen? How is a WASP supposed to understand how the rest of us feel? You already have everything—money and a beautiful house and beautiful parents and a million Travises. Well, I have just one, and I'm not going to let my relationship with him be spoiled by a snobbish WASP."

Karen looked stunned and then said quietly, "You're the snob, not me. You're the one who looks down on people who live on the East Side or who don't speak English, not me. I'm sorry if I ever did anything to make you think otherwise."

She compressed her lips tightly and left the table without another word.

Luisa turned fiercely to Mary Beth. "Don't you say anything. Don't you tell me I'm not being fair to Karen. Or to Travis. Or my parents, or my brother, or Tom."

"Or yourself," Mary Beth said. "Come on, we'll be late to biology."

That night the phone rang three times.

The first time Luisa's uncle Angel called to make arrangements for driving Mami and Luisa to New York on Saturday. Luisa made a point of not complaining about the shopping trip. She figured she had better learn to compromise on the little things, and, besides, the sooner she got the stupid *quince* over with, the sooner Mami and Papi would start leaving her alone a little bit. Going to buy the *quince* dress seemed somehow to hasten the process of turning fifteen.

The second call was from Karen.

"I'm sorry, Karen, I really am," Luisa blurted out, as soon as she recognized Karen's voice.

"I'm sorry, too. But, listen, I have an idea. Why don't you meet Travis at my house this weekend? My parents'll be out Friday night, and I'll just stay in my sister's room, out of sight. You can have the house to yourself."

It seemed too good to be true.

"Because I've been doing a lot of thinking about this," Karen explained, "and I realize that either I'm right and Travis isn't good enough for you, or you're right and he is, and the important thing now is for you to get a chance to be with him for a while—to find out. And, Luisa, you may not believe me, but I really do hope it turns out that I'm wrong."

"I know that—I even knew it the whole time today at lunch—"

"So the house is yours Friday night."

"Would he—does he know where your family lives? I mean, would he know that the house was your house?"

"No," Karen said. "If you want to tell him you live there, that's okay."

But Luisa knew Karen didn't really think it was okay.

"Or you can just say that it's your friend's house, and your friend wants to play Friar Lawrence to Romeo and Juliet."

"If your parents find out you let me have a guy over, won't you be in trouble?" Luisa asked, surprising herself by trying to talk Karen out of her offer.

"I've been in trouble before," Karen said evenly. "So call up old Travis and tell him it's all set."

Luisa called Travis right away. She told him her parents were going to be out Friday night—that they had tickets for a Broadway show—and he could come over if he wanted. In one way, the lie was easy to tell. It seemed natural to treat Karen's English Tudor house as her own. That was where she felt comfortable, where she really belonged. She felt like a misfit in Bridgeport, not Weston.

Travis accepted the invitation gladly, almost too gladly.

Luisa suddenly realized she was asking him to spend hours all alone with her in an empty house. She had assumed they would watch TV or shoot some pool in Karen's carpeted basement, fix themselves a snack, and then curl up on the couch for a while and—well, talk. She hadn't really talked to Travis yet. She hardly knew him, and he didn't know her at all. But now she didn't know if she could take three or four hours of solid making out, no matter how much she loved him. Maybe Karen should invite one of her boyfriends over, too, and they could make up a foursome.

She was lying on the living room rug, debating the merits of this idea, when the phone rang a third time.

Luisa could hear Mami shouting into the receiver in Spanish, as she always did.

"No, no, of course not. I won't tell him that you called me. . . . Yes. . . . Yes. . . . Yes, I thought so. We were worried, but we didn't want you to think we were interfering. . . . Of course you can. . . . How much? . . . No, no, we have enough for the party. You aren't to worry any more. . . . Really. . . . Okay, that's all right. . . . Okay, good-bye, Anna."

Anna, Luisa thought. What was wrong with Roberto and Anna? She glanced over at Papi. He looked angry. Mami put down the receiver and walked into the living room with a half-guilty, half-defiant expression on her face.

"You aren't lending them money for him to lose at jai alai," Papi said.

"I'm not lending it to Roberto. I'm lending it to Anna."

"What happened now?" Papi asked.

Mami looked at Luisa.

"Let her stay," Papi said. "She might as well hear about

it. So what's gone wrong at Roberto's, and how much will it cost us to fix it?"

"It's the grocery money," Mami explained. "Roberto gives Anna fifty dollars a week for groceries, but tonight when he went to the fronton he made Anna open her pocketbook and give all the money to him. He told her he would bring back double, and give all his winnings to Anna and Bobby and never gamble any more."

"So why is Anna all upset?" Papi asked with a mirthless chuckle. "It's just nine o'clock. There's still time tonight for him to win back the grocery money five times over."

"She has no money now to go to the store," Mami said.

"You think the money you give her will go for groceries?" Papi asked scornfully.

"She isn't going to tell him she has it," Mami pleaded. "It's for little Bobby, too, remember."

Papi reached into his pocket, took out his wallet, and counted some bills. "Thirty dollars is plenty for groceries," he said. "For one week they can do without beer and potato chips."

Still shaking his head disapprovingly, he left to start up the van, so that he and Mami could drive over to Anna's before Roberto returned. Luisa listened for the squeak of the brakes, as the van slowly backed into the narrow street. Once they were gone she took out a record of one of the songs she had danced to with Travis. "I can't wait for you to let me love you," the man sang, with a driving, sensual urgency. Luisa wondered if Travis would be able to wait. She had her doubts.

CHAPTER

15

Mami and Papi didn't want to let Luisa go to Karen's on Friday night. Finally, though, she wore them down with her stubborn, gloomy silence. Mami did come out to the front steps, however, to make sure it really was Karen's parents who stopped to pick her up for the evening, and it was, right at seven o'clock. Karen gave Mami a cheery wave from the window, and Mami waved back. Luisa marveled at how much easier it was to get along with other people's parents.

She felt pretty guilty about deceiving Mami and Papi again—especially after Mami had been so understanding the last time—but she felt even worse when Mrs. Cuffner, looking so elegant in a black evening dress, with her hair swept up in an artfully placed comb, gave them her parting instructions: "Leave a little food in the refrigerator to tide us over till morning; don't tie up the phone in case we want to call; no boyfriends over." Luisa glanced at Karen, but Karen just said, as she steered her parents out the door, "Yeah, yeah, and we won't play with matches or stick peas up our nose." Both girls were relieved, however, when the car disappeared down the street.

"I'll be in my sister's room watching TV," Karen said. "There's some made-for-TV movie about a pioneer woman doctor down in Appalachia, and you know how I am about anything having to do with women doctors. Maybe if I watch it I won't feel so panicky about those premed science courses I'll have to take in college."

"Karen," Luisa told her, "anyone who doesn't mind dissecting frogs in biology class—anyone who says, and I quote, 'I think dissections are interesting'—has to end up being a doctor."

Karen laughed. "If you need first aid after a few hours with loverboy Travis, just scream and I'll come running with my little black bag."

"Don't worry," Luisa said, worried half sick herself.

At a quarter to eight the doorbell rang. Luisa peeked out the front living room window: The blue Mustang was parked in the driveway. Okay, she told herself, okay. She opened the door, and Travis stood there, his football jacket open, smiling at her.

"Hi," she said, trying to sound natural. "Come on in."

"So this is the mighty fortress where the dragons guard Luisa," he said, looking around at the living room with an appraising eye. Luisa followed his glance and took in, as if for the first time, the thick pale-blue carpeting and deeper blue velour sofa, formed of three detachable sections. A fourth was on the other side of the simple, modern glass coffee table, next to the blue-flowered armchair Karen's parents had just had reupholstered by Luisa's. The large picture over the fireplace was an abstract: Blue and brown swirled together in a way that made Luisa think of the sea meeting the sand. There were real seascapes, too, that Karen's parents had bought from local artists on Martha's Vineyard, where they had a weekend cottage. And there wasn't a single crucifix anywhere. She giggled, and Travis looked at her inquiringly.

"I'm just happy," she explained.

"That's good," he said, and he put his arm around her shoulders.

"Are you hungry?" she asked, glad she knew her way perfectly around the Cuffners' kitchen, with its bright display of copper cookware and bunches of onions and gourds carefully hanging from stout wooden beams.

"No, I just finished eating supper a little while ago. Besides, the coach thinks it's a bad idea to eat a lot the night before a game."

"Well, if you want anything later, let me know," Luisa said, and then, suddenly, she stopped. She was behaving just like Mami! Someone walked in the door, and, bingo! food all over the place. She swallowed hard and asked, "Is it a tough game tomorrow?"

"You'd better believe it," he groaned, and then launched into a detailed account of football strategy. Luisa didn't understand a word of it—football wasn't exactly the hottest thing going at Our Lady of the Mountains, and Papi and Abuelo spent all their excitement on the World Series—but she tried to look interested. She said "Yeah" and "Uh-huh" and "Ummm" whenever there was a pause in the conversation—or rather, the monologue. But she guessed she was doing okay because it was ten minutes or so—at the very least, she thought—before he shrugged good-naturedly and said, "Come on, don't let me bore you." Her face had begun to feel a little stiff from the fixed expression of attentiveness. "How about you? Did you learn any new prayers at school this week?"

"No," Luisa answered, trying unsuccessfully to think of a witty response. She wished she weren't so sensitive about her religion. "Just more quadratic equations to factor, and the plundering of Carthage in world history."

"Are all your teachers nuns?"

"Yes. We had a man teacher, Mr. Berrigan, for physics and chemistry last year, but too many of the girls had crushes on him, so he had to go."

"Did you have a crush on this Berrigan guy?"

"No," Luisa lied. She had spent weeks poring over the chemistry book on her own, despairing because she couldn't take chemistry until she was a junior.

"Do you have a crush on me?" Travis asked, pulling her closer to him on the couch. Their eyes met.

"Yes," she whispered, and they kissed.

Luisa wished she liked kissing Travis more. If you were in love with someone, she reasoned, while he pressed his lips against hers and forced his tongue inside her mouth, you shouldn't keep counting how many seconds have to go by until it can be over. Certainly after sixty she could stop for a breather.

"Would you like to play pool?" Luisa asked, pulling her face away.

Travis looked startled. "Sure," he said, a little uncertainly. "Do you play much?"

They filed downstairs to the paneled basement. "A little," she said. "I mean, it's mostly my brother who plays."

Actually, Luisa had won a city-wide pool tournament when she was eleven. She had practically lived in the recreation room at Karen's house back then, shooting balls into pockets over and over again. She had hated to give it up, but she couldn't see herself competing in pool halls all over the state once she was in her teens. It wouldn't have been the most feminine thing in the world.

"Here," Travis said, picking up the blue chalk. "You have to chalk up first." He did his own cue first, then took hers and chalked it, too. Luisa didn't say anything.

"I better break," he said. He did an okay job, Luisa decided, evaluating his performance with a critical eye. Not terrific, but okay.

It was her turn. She almost said, "Number fourteen to the corner pocket," but stopped herself in time. The number fourteen ball slammed into the pocket, anyway, just as she had planned.

"Way to go!" Travis said encouragingly. "Why don't

you try the orange-striped ball, over there?" Luisa looked. The number seven was definitely better. With a swift movement she sent it flying against the number nine, and nodded with calm satisfaction as the nine followed the fourteen.

Travis didn't look so happy this time. "You've played 'a little'?" he asked.

Luisa grinned as she scored again. "Maybe a lot."

When Travis's turn came he was visibly ill at ease. He barely grazed the first ball with the cue. It rolled a few inches. "Try again," Luisa urged. He scowled, and then smashed the ball so hard that it bounced over the rim of the table and rolled across the floor. Luisa wanted to laugh, but Travis looked mad. She missed the next time, on purpose, and he seemed a little relieved, but Luisa was beginning to realize that the pool playing had been a bad idea.

"Let's not play any more," she said. "It's probably not good for your muscles if you're in training for football."

"Pool," Travis said, "takes absolutely no muscles at all." But he laid down the pool cue willingly and followed her back upstairs.

It was only eight forty-five.

"There's a movie on TV at nine," Luisa said.

"What movie?" Travis asked, without much interest.

"It's about this lady who was a doctor down in Appalachia. She was one of the first women in the country to be a doctor, back in the late 1800s, I think."

"Sounds boring as hell," Travis said. "I didn't realize you were that much of a women's libber."

"I'm not," Luisa said, wondering what in the world could have given him that idea. Just that she was interested in a pioneer woman doctor and that she beat him at one crummy game of pool? Well, she did call him on the phone, she remembered. And she didn't think it was fair that Mami and Papi treated her different from Joey, that they had a double standard for dating curfews and housework. But Travis didn't even know about that. If all those things made her a "women's libber," then she guessed she was one. But she didn't like the way Travis said it. In fact, she wasn't sure right then that she liked Travis himself all that much, either.

"Hey," he said gently. She sat stiffly, staring at the blank TV screen, refusing to turn and look at him.

"Hey, don't be mad." He got up and squatted down on the floor directly in front of her so that she couldn't avoid meeting his gaze.

"Why shouldn't I be?" she asked, feeling her disappointment evaporate too quickly.

"I bet you think I'm a poor sport. You think I just can't stand to be beaten by a girl."

"Well . . ." Luisa began, wanting to deny the truth of what he said, but unable to make a lie sound at all convincing. They both noticed her hesitation and laughed.

"Okay, you're right. I *am* a poor sport. And it's not just being beaten by a weak, scrawny, little—"

"Wait a minute!" Luisa protested. "I did win, remember."

"Girl," he finished, grinning. "I hate being beaten by anyone. In sports, that is."

"Your football team doesn't win all that much," Luisa observed, unable to resist.

"Don't I know it. But they don't lose because of me. No one could give it any more than I do."

"You!"

"Yes, me. Why so surprised? If you ever came to the

games you'd see what football heroes are made of. No, honestly, I'm good. Not great, but good."

"Why not great?"

"What I'm great in is baseball. I'm a great pitcher."

"And so modest, too," she teased.

Travis looked troubled. "If I tell you something, will you promise not to tell my father?"

"I don't even know your father."

"I know, but listen—aw, you're going to think this is stupid. . . ."

"No, tell me."

"Well, what I really want to do after I graduate is—well, I don't want to go to college at all. Not to any of those places I told you about the other night. I think—well, there's a good chance that I'll get a draft from a ball club. The Red Sox had a scout out here last spring to watch me play, and I think he liked what he saw. And if they make me an offer, I want to take it."

"So take it," Luisa said. "You have to take it." She loved him, after all. They *could* share things. And Travis did care passionately about something.

"My father would have ten thousand fits. He'd die or disown me—I can't even think of what he'd do, it'd be so terrible. He wants me to be a big hot-shot corporation lawyer like he is. And I just want to play ball."

"My brother Joey is the same way," Luisa said, trying to think of something she could say that would show him she understood. "My father wants Joey to work for him, but all Joey wants is to be on his own."

"What does your father do?"

"He has—he's in reupholstery."

"And your brother wants to be—"

"Anything else."

"It sounds like he and I would get along. That is, if he

keeps out of my way in my dealings with his sister."

He kissed her again, and began fondling her breasts under her blouse. They eased into a reclining position on the blue velour couch—Luisa kept hoping Travis's gym shoes wouldn't get the cushions dirty—and kissed some more, their bodies pressed together. Luisa could feel her breasts flattened against Travis's hard chest, and her hips flush against his.

"What time are they coming back?" Travis murmured, running his hand up her thigh, under her skirt.

Luisa wanted to tell him they were coming back any minute, but he knew that she wouldn't have invited him over for such a short time.

"I don't know," she said. "Eleven o'clock, maybe."

"I thought they were going to catch a show down in the city."

"Something came up at the last minute," she said, fumbling for an excuse.

"That's okay, we have plenty of time." He moved his hand up her thigh a little higher. Luisa felt a strange, disturbing, exciting tingle.

"I told you that night at the dance," she began. She could feel her heart pounding.

"You don't have to be afraid," he said. "I won't hurt you."

"I'm just not ready for anything too—heavy."

"I understand," he whispered, but he didn't take his hand away from her leg.

"Please don't," she finally said, and pushed it away gently.

"Doesn't it feel good?" he asked.

"It feels wonderful," Luisa answered. "But I just don't want to do it."

To her relief he seemed to accept her decision philosophically. He kissed her some more and even agreed to watch the rest of the movie. Luisa knew Karen must be loving every minute of it: The doctor was so beautiful and determined and noble. She could hardly wait to talk about it with her later. She wanted to talk to Travis more, too, about baseball and what he could do to make his parents realize how much it meant to him to play professionally, but she didn't know how to reintroduce the subject. So she didn't say anything else about it.

The movie was over at eleven o'clock. Travis stretched and yawned a little. "I guess I'd better be shoving off," he said. "I don't want to cut it too close with your folks or anything."

"You're probably right," Luisa agreed.

"Some friends of mine are having a party tomorrow night after the game. Any chance you could make it?"

Luisa sighed, this time with real regret. She would love to walk into a party with Travis and have everyone there know that she was with him, his girl friend, even. But there was no way Mami and Papi would let her go out both Friday and Saturday night. "I wish I could," she said, "but I already made other plans." Like for watching Spanish situation comedies on TV.

"Well, give me a call during the week sometime," he said, tossing his car keys from one hand to the other. "Wednesday would be good."

He gave her a last kiss and went out to the car. Luisa watched from the window and wondered why she didn't feel more of a pang as he backed out of the driveway and drove away.

CHAPTER

16

Karen looked surprised when Luisa burst into her sister's room at a few minutes past eleven, asking excitedly, "Aren't you twice as inspired now?" She stared at her friend without comprehension. "I mean, after the movie," Luisa added. "You did watch the movie, didn't you?"

"Yes," Karen said. "But somehow I didn't think you and Travis would. It doesn't sound like his idea of a Friday night."

"It was my idea," Luisa confessed.

"Is everything okay?"

"Yes, sure," Luisa said, "but I think we ought to start getting you ready for med school. And tell your parents you need riding lessons for your birthday. A horse will come in handy down in Appalachia."

"Do my ears deceive me?" Karen asked. "Or did you come in here after your second date with the most fabulous guy in the universe to talk about my career?"

"Well, it's a very interesting topic of conversation, don't you think?" Luisa flopped onto the bed next to Karen, who propped herself up on one elbow to study Luisa more closely.

"Okay, I give up. What's going on?" she asked.

"Nothing, really. I'm just in a strange mood."

"You're telling *me!* So what did happen with loverboy? Do you like him more or less than you did three hours ago?"

"More, I think. I guess I know him better. He's more sensitive than most people realize—he has a lot of dreams and secret doubts that he doesn't usually talk to people about."

"But he talked about them to you?"

"Yes, he did. At least he made a start. It wasn't easy for him, either, but I think he's learning that he can trust me to listen and not laugh at him."

"And what about you?"

"What *about* me?"

"Did you tell him all your dreams and secret doubts?"

"No, but then again, I don't really have any."

Karen didn't say anything.

"I don't."

"If you don't have them, then I'd hate to meet someone who did. But, okay, here's *my* dream and secret doubt: My dream is that there's still some chocolate cake in the refrigerator, and my secret doubt is that you and Travis ate it all."

Luisa threw the pillow at her. "That's right, make fun of Travis and me, go ahead," she sniffed. But she wasn't at all mad. She had survived a whole evening alone with Travis; she hadn't let him pressure her into going much farther with him sexually; she knew he still liked her, because he had asked her to the party tomorrow night. And, whatever Karen might say, he had opened himself up to her, showing her that he thought she was somebody special. And he seemed more special himself, too. At least she felt she knew him better now.

Luckily, Karen's dream came true: There was a whole half of the chocolate layer cake in the kitchen. Karen cut herself a thick wedge.

"I'm just going to have an itsy-bitsy slice," Luisa announced. But when she was done with the first itsy-bitsy slice, she shaved off a second, and then a third and a fourth.

"Mary Beth says it's less fattening this way," she ex-

plained, pressing the moist, dark crumbs on her plate together with her fork.

"That guy from the dance ever call her?" Karen asked.
"I don't like to keep bugging her about him if he's a lost
cause, but I was really hoping that this time—"

"I know. Me, too."

"You met him, didn't you?"

Luisa nodded. "Twice," she said, with her mouth full
of cake.

"So what do you think? How much of a chance is
there?"

Luisa swallowed. "It's hard to say. I think he likes her,
I really do. It seemed that way to me at the dance, and
then when I saw him at the diner he made a big deal
about my saying hello to her. But he still hasn't called
her. I've stopped asking her about it, too, because she just
says all that stuff about not wanting a boyfriend, anyway,
and how it's more fun to help me with my boyfriends—
you know Mary Beth."

"This Doug—he couldn't just be shy, could he?"

"Maybe. He's the shy type, basically, from what I've
seen. That's why he's so perfect for Mary Beth."

"Why doesn't she follow your fine example?"

"What do you mean?"

"She could call him, you know. Sometimes it's not only
right; it's necessary."

"That's true, but what if he really isn't interested?
Think how terrible she'd feel."

"Well, think how terrible *he'd* feel if he called her and
she wasn't interested."

"Okay, then, Mary Beth is going to call him. Tonight.
He's probably getting home from the diner just about
now." Luisa pointed to the phone. Plans such as this were

not noted for surviving scrutiny in the morning light, so it seemed best to act now. "Should you call her, or should I?"

"You do it. I'll help you out on the extension upstairs."

Luisa felt a twinge of misgiving when she realized by the slow bewilderment of Mrs. Murphy's "Hello?" that she had awakened Mary Beth's mother. But Mary Beth sounded alert and wide awake when she came to the phone, and the idea seemed brilliant again.

"How was it?" Mary Beth whispered.

"Mary Beth," Luisa said, "Karen and I have decided that as soon as we hang up you are going to call Doug and ask him out."

"You didn't call me in the middle of the night to tell me that, did you?"

"We most certainly did," Luisa said.

"So is it all set? Are you going to do it?" Karen asked.

"He likes you, Mary Beth. You should have heard him at the diner," Luisa said.

"Someone has to take the initiative," Karen said.

"And that someone is you," Luisa said.

"Wait a minute," Mary Beth said. "What makes you guys think I want to go out with him in the first place, or with anyone, for that matter?"

"Do you know his number?" Karen asked.

"It's in the phone book."

"Are you sure? Look it up," Luisa said.

"I looked it up once before."

Luisa and Karen waited, holding their breath.

"But if I did call him, what would I say?"

"You'd say, 'Hello, Doug. This is Mary Beth, the girl from the dance. I just called up to say hello,'" Luisa proposed.

"At midnight I just called up to say hello?"

"Then you'd say, 'I would have called you earlier to-night, but Luisa told me you were working at the diner. She gave me your message.' "

"And then what?"

"You'd say you were wondering if he'd like to go to a movie tomorrow night or next weekend or whenever he has a day off."

"And he'd say, 'Nope, sorry, I wouldn't.' "

"No, he wouldn't," Karen said. "And even if he did, you never have to see him again. It's not as if he's in all your classes at Our Lady, right?"

"Come on, we'll practice," Luisa said. "I'll be Doug. 'Hello?' "

"No, let's not practice."

"But you'll call him?"

"I'll call him. But just so the two of you will finally get off my case."

"Good luck," Luisa said, and, before Mary Beth could change her mind or lose her nerve, quickly hung up. Then, cheering strenuously, she bounded up the stairs to where Karen was waiting.

"We did it!" she shouted, leaping on top of Karen on her parents' double bed and giving her a bear hug. She tossed one of the pillows up in the air. "Hip!" She tossed the other. "Hip!" She grabbed the third, but then stopped. She picked up the receiver and dialed Mary Beth's number. The line was busy, and Luisa aimed the third pillow. "Hooray!" she finished.

They returned to Karen's sister's room to watch a "Honeymooners" rerun while waiting for Mary Beth's call. Ralph Kramden had already been caught by Alice in a lie about going bowling with the boys. She had forgiven him everything, and he had said, "Alice, you're the great-est." Ed Norton was just going through an elaborate ceremony of tucking in his napkin in the concluding minute of the program, when the phone finally rang.

Luisa got to it first.

"I did it, and we're going out next weekend," Mary Beth said, before Luisa could even say hello.

"He told me he wanted to call me, but he'd never called a girl before, can you believe it? He said he was sure someone like me had a boyfriend already. He said he didn't know what he'd have done if he hadn't bumped into you at the diner."

"Oh," Luisa said sadly, clucking her tongue against her teeth. "It's such a shame you aren't interested in going out with anybody. And it sounds like going out with Doug might have been so much fun, too."

"I never said anything of the sort," Mary Beth protested, laughing.

"I wish I had a tape recorder. You said that all that mattered to you was just being the brain behind my romance with Travis."

"Well, if I hadn't been tracking Travis with you, I wouldn't have been at the Trumbull dance in the first place. And, besides, I meant a lot of that, I really did. Because boyfriends may be fun—but you've got to admit they're a lot of trouble, too."

"Girls?" Karen's mother suddenly called from the front entrance hall. In all the excitement neither Karen nor Luisa had heard the car. "We're home!"

Luisa hung up the phone then and slipped on her jacket, so that the Cuffners could drive her home right away. She'd have to be up bright and early to drive down to New York with Angel and Mami. It had been an exhausting evening—and maybe that showed that Mary Beth wasn't so wrong about boyfriends, after all.

17

There was no *quince* shopping trip the next day. Luisa and Mami were waiting in the kitchen for Angel to pick them up, already arguing about what kind of dress would be appropriate for a fifteen-year-old, when the phone rang. "It's Consuela," Mami grumbled good-naturedly, reaching for the receiver, "to tell us that her lazy, good-for-nothing husband is still snoring away in his bed."

But it was Anna. "What is wrong? What is the matter?" Mami asked her. "Anna, you have to pull yourself together if I'm going to understand what you're saying. Start again from the beginning." She answered Luisa's inquiring look with a bewildered shrug. "Anna? Anna? Hello? Anna?" She tapped the receiver bar several times. "Hello? Anna?"

"She hung up on me," Mami said slowly, replacing the receiver.

"Do you think Roberto made her give him that grocery money Papi lent her?" Luisa asked.

"I don't know. But if he put a hand on her—" Mami finished the sentence by gesturing with her fist. "Go call your father and brother, baby. I'll leave a note for Angel. Anna needs us."

Papi was still sleeping and Joey was fifteen minutes into one of his marathon showers, but in another fifteen minutes they were both dressed. "This is the third time in a week that we're going to Roberto's," Papi observed, as Mami knelt down to lace his work shoes. "Do they think the rest of us have nothing better to do?"

"Oh, be quiet," Mami snapped. "He's your own brother."

Papi might complain, but he lost no time in driving to Anna's, and half ran up the stairs as Luisa and Joey followed right behind him, while Mami, puffing and panting, brought up the rear. Bobby opened to Papi's emphatic knock. His face was streaked with tears, as well as peanut butter and jelly. But, of course, Bobby was usually crying.

Inside, they found Anna huddled in an armchair, the new, expensive armchair whose pale-beige upholstery she kept carefully covered by a clear plastic slipcover. She, who was usually so meticulous about her appearance, looked a mess. Metal curlers sprouted all over her head, not even covered by a kerchief. Her housedress was half unbuttoned, and some of her flabby stomach showed through. Her nose needed wiping almost as much as Bobby's did. Luisa ached with pity for her, and embarrassment that she should look like that in front of Papi and Joey.

"I am so ashamed," she kept moaning. "I am so ashamed."

Papi sounded unusually gentle. "What is it, Anna?" he asked in a low voice. "What has happened?"

She shook her head, and a great gasping sob escaped her.

"Did my brother hit you? Has he done anything to hurt you?" He shook her arm. "Anna! You have to tell us so that we can help you."

"In the closet," Anna said.

Papi took a step toward the linen closet in the hallway.

"The bedroom closet," Anna whispered, and hid her face in her hands.

Bewildered, Papi led the way to Roberto and Anna's bedroom. The closet door stood open. Papi and Joey looked inside, not knowing what they were looking for, and seeing nothing. Papi turned to Mami helplessly, and he and Joey moved aside so she and Luisa could have a look. It was just an ordinary closet. The conservative suits Roberto wore to the World Trade Center hung neatly in the back, and Anna's gaily flowered dresses and polyester pantsuits in the front. A plaid flannel bathrobe and a sheer, gauzy negligee robe hung side by side on two hooks on the inside of the door. Shoe boxes were stacked in piles on the floor.

All of a sudden Luisa knew, with a sickening realization, why Anna was crying. The top shoe box was unlike the others. It was old and battered, held together with masking tape that was peeling off. Luisa knew there were no shoes in that box. There wasn't any money, either, although there had been. Jaime's money.

"The shoe box," she just said.

Mami looked at the floor of the closet. "Oh, my God," she said slowly. "Oh, my God."

They heard a sound behind them. Anna stood in the doorway, watching them with a kind of grim satisfaction. "His own father-in-law," she said. "My own father, who gives us the roof over our heads."

"Are you sure that's the same shoe box?" Joey asked lamely.

Anna nodded, her fact twisted with misery. "His own father-in-law," she repeated. "His own father-in-law. His own—" Papi put his arms around her, and she collapsed against him. He led her to the living room sofa and sat beside her, mechanically patting her hand. Nobody said anything. Everyone just waited. Any minute, Roberto should be coming home with Jaime from the grocery store. The only sound in the room was Anna's quiet crying and the wheeze of the old refrigerator.

Luisa could think of nothing but her disappointment in Roberto. How could he—the most assimilated, the most "American" of her relatives—do such a thing? All right, he didn't have Miguel's money, and his restaurant had failed where Miguel's had succeeded. But Luisa considered him in some ways far more successful than Miguel: It was almost impossible to tell that Roberto was an immigrant. And however dissatisfied he might be with his own situation, there was no excuse for this—this betrayal of his own family. She couldn't imagine being comfortable with him, her favorite uncle, her godfather, ever again.

They heard a car door slam, and the indistinct sounds of male voices. Then, Roberto's quick, sure footsteps on the stairs. He looked surprised and pleased to see them all, and gave Joey a friendly slap on the back when Joey automatically relieved him of the heavy sacks of groceries. But when he saw Anna's tears and Papi's unsmiling face, his expression changed.

"Have you been crying to my family again?" he shouted.

"We found Jaime's shoe box," Papi said as if he were merely communicating a fact.

"It was in your closet," Papi went on. "The money in it was all gone."

Anna burst out, "How could you? Roberto, how could you? How could you steal from him?"

Roberto finished lighting his cigarette. "I didn't steal it," he said quietly. "I just borrowed it for a little while. I'm going to return it to him, all of it, with interest. Why should money sit in a shoe box when it could be making even more money?"

"Better it sit in the closet forever than go to the pockets of those crooks at the jai alai," Mami said. "When are you going to repay it? The next time you win the trifecta?"

Luisa knew that she and Joey were supposed to keep still and not interfere, but she was too angry and disgusted with Roberto to control herself. "Jaime cried when he couldn't find his money," she said. "He *cried*."

"An old man who loves you and trusts you," Anna wept. Roberto's face was tight and impassive. It was impossible to tell if he felt angry or ashamed or completely indifferent to their words. Then suddenly he turned away, and his shoulders heaved with dry sobs. Luisa had never seen a man cry. Roberto's hysterical collapse frightened and sickened her. She couldn't believe those horrible, almost animallike noises were coming from her smooth, sophisticated, college-educated, English-speaking uncle.

"You—don't—know—anything," Roberto finally managed to say, once the spasms had subsided.

"We're listening," Papi said unsympathetically. And then Roberto started in with his story.

It was much worse than Luisa could have imagined. Roberto had been losing steadily now for some weeks. On occasional lucky nights he recovered part of his losses, but he just turned around and poured his winnings back into jai alai, determined to win big—big enough to cancel out all the humiliating losses, big enough to be able to boast that he had beaten jai alai, after all. His savings—all the money he had put away to buy a house in the suburbs and to send Bobby to college—had gone first, the work of three or four desperate evenings. He had begun borrowing money next, from Angel and Consuela, from the neighbors in back, and some of the men at work. Finally he had written himself a phony check for a thousand dollars against the company account, planning to win enough money with it to discharge all his debts and return the money to the company coffers before anyone could notice it was missing. But he just kept on losing. So last Saturday morning, while Jaime was at Lou's, he had hurried downstairs, let himself into Jaime's ground-floor apartment with his own key, and headed right for the closet where he knew the money was hidden. In a minute he had added Jaime's shoe box to the pile in his closet and pocketed the cash. With this money, he would win back all the rest: Just one lucky evening, and it would be as if nothing had gone wrong.

There was a stunned silence when he finished talking.

"Did you lose all of Jaime's money at jai alai?" Luisa whispered.

Roberto nodded, without meeting her eyes.

"But you knew we would find the shoe box there; you must have known it," Mami said.

"I need someone to help me," Roberto said brokenly. "I can't go on like this any more. Somebody has to help me."

"Nobody can help you unless you help yourself," Papi said. "The first thing you have to do is swear you will never go near the jai alai fronton again."

"But then all that money is gone—gone! If I go just one more time I can win it all back—"

"How can you still say that?" Papi shouted. "You are supposed to be so smart, you with your college degree. How can you be so stupid? If all this hasn't taught you a lesson, what will it take to teach you?"

"I have to pay back Angel and Jaime and all the others," Roberto insisted dully. "If I do not have the thousand dollars by the end of this week the accountant will find that it is missing, and they will take me to court. I will lose my job, and everyone will know what a fool I've been—" His voice broke.

"You can pay it back," Papi said, "but penny by penny. Fortunes don't accumulate overnight, at jai alai or anywhere else."

"But Miguel—"

"Forget Miguel! Forget him! I lost money in the restaurant, too, as much as you, more than you, and I've forgotten it. Why can't you?"

"I'm finished," Roberto said, cradling his head in his hands. "I don't know what to do anymore, where to begin."

"I'll help you," Papi promised grimly. "But only if you do everything I say and stay away from the fronton."

He motioned to the bedroom, and the two men went in together, Papi with his arm around Roberto's shoulders, and shut the door behind them. Sometime during Roberto's confession Bobby had switched on the television, and Luisa was suddenly aware of Fred Flintstone's "Yabadabadoo!" on the Saturday morning cartoons. A commercial for Cocoa Puffs came on and one for Hostess Twinkies.

"I'll help you fix some lunch," Mami told Anna, "after I call Angel and Consuela. We were supposed to go to New York today."

Anna looked at Mami fearfully. "You don't have to tell them—everything," she pleaded. Mami smiled reassuringly, but Luisa knew that everyone in Bridgeport, Miami, Key West—maybe even Cuba—would know before the week was over. News traveled quickly, good and bad, but bad news traveled faster. When Luisa's cousin in

Miami, Miguel's son, had been busted for possession of marijuana, the Bridgeport community had known within half an hour. Luisa and Joey weren't supposed to tell their friends things like that, not even Tom and Mary Beth, but they themselves were always told. It was just family.

By the time Papi and Roberto emerged from the bedroom, Mami had prepared a platter of sandwiches and Anna had combed out her hair, buttoned up her housedress, and put on some lipstick. "I'm starving," Roberto said, rubbing his hands together with a hollow heartiness, trying to make everything seem normal again. "What do you say we eat?"

Luisa had thought she was starving, too, but the thick roast beef sandwich she took seemed tasteless and dry, and she left the better part of it untouched on her plate.

CHAPTER

18 By Sunday morning it was beginning to look as if there would not only be no *quince* shopping trip—there would not even be much of a *quince*. Papi had agreed to lend Roberto the thousand dollars to repay his debt at work before it was discovered. The condition was that Roberto sign his paycheck over to Papi each week, so that Papi could supervise the gradual repayment of the other debts—and so that Roberto wouldn't have any cash to gamble away at jai alai. So the dinner dance at the Cuban Club was off. There would be just a little party for family and friends at 446 Tilden Street.

Luisa was surprised at how disappointed she felt. She had told them all along that she didn't want a big fuss made over her, but it would have been fun to wear a formal gown and dance to the music of a live band. If only things had been different, she could even have danced with Travis—not fast dances like at the Trumbull dance, but waltzes and foxtrots. It would have been so romantic. But of course Travis would never have wanted to go to the Bridgeport Cuban Club, to a Spanish *quince* celebration. She could have danced with Tom, though. She could tell that he would be a good dancer.

But Luisa wasn't about to complain. She felt so sorry for Anna, and even for Roberto—and she felt proud of Mami and Papi for sticking by him. She remembered other things about her parents, too, that she had almost forgotten. Before her other grandfather, Papi's father, had died three years ago, he had been sick for a long, long time. Mami and Papi had never even thought of letting him go away to a nursing home. Not that they could have afforded one if they *had* considered it. But they hadn't. They had taken him in to live with them, and Mami had fed and bathed him and run back and forth with the bedpan, even when he cursed her or lay sullen and silent. When it came right down to it, Mami and Papi were okay. Too loud and too fat and too Cuban, but okay.

She didn't even grumble—much—when Mami asked her if she would mind taking Joey's place on an afternoon reupholstery delivery. Joey was working at Victor's, and Mami herself, who usually went with Papi when Joey couldn't, was in bed with a stomachache. I should think she'd have a stomachache, Luisa thought, after eating that whole bucket of Kentucky Fried Chicken last night.

The couch to be delivered wasn't heavy, just awkward, and even if it were, it would be just as heavy for Mami as for Luisa. Luisa thought about the pictures of Mami's wedding again. The pretty young bride in the photographs certainly hadn't realized she was soon going to find herself hauling reupholstered furniture all over creation in a secondhand van. No, Luisa couldn't imagine Mami being all that thrilled about going on the deliveries, either. From now on she was going to help Mami and Papi more. Wasn't that what families were all about?

"Don't worry, I'll go with Papi," she agreed, now feeling almost cheerful about it. "You just rest. And try not to eat anything."

She and Papi loaded the couch into the van: It was an antique, upholstered in an elegant, expensive, pale-pink sprigged satin. Definitely not the kind of couch teen-age kids were meant to sprawl on. One buttery handful of popcorn, one melting Popsicle, and the couch would be ruined. It probably belonged to some little old lady, she speculated, as they rattled north on the Merritt Parkway.

The delivery was in Trumbull, and whenever Luisa thought of Trumbull, she thought of Travis. She wondered what he would think about Roberto and jai alai. For all she knew, he might have an uncle or cousin with the same problem, because Roberto really was the least "Bridgeport" and the most "Trumbull" of her relatives. If Travis did have a relative like Roberto, how would his parents react? All Luisa knew of Mr. Blaine was his deep businesslike telephone voice, and Mrs. Blaine she could only picture as the twin of Harold's slim mother. Would they immediately offer this relative whatever he needed to straighten out his life, even if they had to sacrifice to do it? Even if it meant dropping out of the country club? And what would Travis do about a Roberto? Even though Luisa had known him for quite a while now— well, almost three weeks—and knew him in some ways so intimately, in other ways she didn't know him at all.

The street they were now driving down, a broad, tree-lined avenue with attractively landscaped houses set well back from the road, looked familiar. Luisa was sure she had been down this street before, and then she remembered it was Harold's street, and the sprawling stone house on the left was Harold's. Poor old Harold. His mother must have been disappointed when she and Mary Beth hadn't come by again.

The owner of the pink satin sofa lived three blocks from Harold, in a handsome dark-green house with cream-colored shutters. A few dried leaves clung to the branches of the enormous old oak trees in front, but the lawn was bare. Every leaf had been raked up and neatly bagged for pickup. Luisa waited in the van while Papi rang the bell. A middle-aged woman with frosted ash-blond hair came to the door, and Papi exchanged a few words with her. Then he returned to the van, sliding the door open with an emphatic bang. Luisa sprang down lightly from the high front seat, and together they lifted the sofa onto the lawn, being careful to keep the pale-pink fabric from touching the sides of the van. Luisa picked up her end and helped Papi carry the sofa up the front steps, and then, tilting the end slightly, through the narrow front door.

"Over here, by the piano," a male voice directed. A familiar male voice.

Luisa stopped. She didn't need to look at him, because she would have known that voice anywhere, but her gaze was involuntarily drawn in his direction, and to her horrified surprise, she found herself looking right into Travis's blue eyes.

Luisa didn't wait to learn how Travis felt about finding his "Weston" girl friend helping her undershirt-clad Cuban dad make a delivery. Abruptly she dropped her end of the couch, and, without a word, turned and ran. "Luisa!" she heard Papi shout, but she kept going, glad as she had never been before that she could sprint a hundred meters in fifteen seconds flat.

"Luisa! Hey, Luisa, wait!"

It was Travis, pounding down the pavement after her. She didn't look back. She wasn't going to let him confront her with all the lies she had told him and all the truths she had left unsaid. Now that he knew everything she had struggled so hard to hide, he could just call one of those glamorous girls he had played volleyball with. He didn't have to bother with her ever again.

Travis ran fast, but Luisa ran faster. He might be a big football hero, but, as he himself had pointed out, she was no mean athelete herself. Spics are just natural-born jocks, anyway, she thought, with a last burst of bitterness. Her headstart was too great, and after another block he had no chance of overtaking her.

She ran past Harold's house—the blue Mustang was now in the driveway—and then through a confusing network of side streets. She didn't know where she was going, and she didn't care. A church, another church. There was a dull pain in her side, and her breath came in short, sharp gasps. She kept running but slowed her pace. "Over here, by the piano. Over here, by the piano. Over here, by the piano." Would she ever stop hearing those words? "Stop it!" she said aloud, to herself and to that insistent inner voice. Well, Karen and Mary Beth and Joey and Tom had all been right. This was what she got for lying. But, she told herself defensively, if she hadn't lied maybe she wouldn't have had any of it.

Down the next side street to the left, the trees and grass turned after another block or two into blacktop, and Luisa could see the backs of the stores of the Trumbull shopping center. She wanted to keep running, to put more distance between her and the excruciating memory of her humiliation, but she felt a painful blister on her big toe from her new wedgie shoes. She limped slowly across the parking lot to the mall.

There was an old, tattered phone book chained to the shelf in the first phone booth Luisa came across. She looked up Victor's Pizzeria. She shouldn't call Tom at work. Victor's might be real busy this afternoon, and she might get him in trouble. Or he might get mad at her for bothering him. But it wouldn't hurt to dial the number, would it?

The phone rang twice. "Victor's Pizzeria," Tom said. By the grateful relief that swept over her, Luisa realized how much she had counted on having Tom answer the phone. There was no one else in the world she wanted to talk to.

"Tom?"

"Lu! What's up?"

"Nothing."

But Tom knew she wouldn't call him at work just to talk.

"Are you okay?"

Luisa couldn't answer, for the tears choking her.

"Where are you?"

"Trumbull," she managed to get out.

"Shopping center?"

"Uh-huh."

"I have a delivery there in a little while. Wait for me at the entrance by the bagel place. Okay? Got it?"

"You don't have to come," Luisa said, hoping desperately that he wouldn't believe her.

"Twenty minutes, then." The receiver clicked.

It seemed closer to half an hour, but finally the Victor's Volkswagen, with Tom at the wheel, pulled up in front of the mall. She suddenly loved him so much, with the deep, overreaching love she felt for Mami, Papi, and Joey.

"Oh, Tom!" She flung her arms around him, and he held her tightly, patting her back gently and kissing her hair.

"Do you want to talk about it?" he asked.

She nodded. "But you should be driving back to Victor's."

He put the VW into gear and she started talking. The words tumbled over one another, and the whole story wasn't long in telling. When she had finished, they were home, home at Tilden Street. Tom was quiet for a while.

"I bet he went running after you because he cares about you," he finally said. "This guy sounds all right to me."

"I can never face him again. That's all there is to it."

"If you're really serious about what you're saying, then I don't see how the relationship can mean all that much to you."

"I guess—" Luisa began, surprised at herself. "I guess maybe it doesn't. I mean, we've had one real conversation so far and even that was all about him. He doesn't know the first thing about me."

"You haven't exactly helped him out much," Tom observed dryly.

"It isn't that I haven't wanted to. I guess I just can't talk to him—not the way I can talk to you. All we do is make out," Luisa blurted, "and—oh, I shouldn't be telling you this, but I don't have anyone else to tell—I don't even *like* kissing him. It's horrible. I'd just as soon kiss *you*—"

Tom grimaced, and Luisa blushed. "I didn't mean it like that. I mean, I really would like to kiss you."

"Would you?" Tom demanded teasingly.

"Sure."

Their faces were very close. "Would you?" he asked again, softly. She could feel his hand tighten on hers—she didn't remember when they had started holding hands—but she returned the pressure.

"Yes," she answered, even more softly.

Then his mouth was on hers, firm and moist and tender, and she responded naturally, without thought or hesitation.

CHAPTER

19

Mami was asleep when Luisa came in. She could tell by the rhythmic snores. The van wasn't in the driveway, which meant Papi wasn't home yet. Luisa threw herself facedown on the couch and buried her face in the lumpy old cushions. But as soon as she closed her eyes, she saw Travis's blue eyes staring into hers. She couldn't make them go away.

She knew that she must have embarrassed Papi terribly in front of an important customer. There was to have been a whole series of heirloom antiques reupholstered after the pink satin sofa, but maybe Mrs. Blaine, afraid of a hysterical scene with every delivery, would cancel the rest of her order. Maybe Luisa had even damaged the delicate curved leg of the sofa when she dropped it. Afterward Mrs. Blaine would have asked Travis, "Who was that dreadful girl? Not one of your friends, I hope," and what would he have said? "Oh, nobody special. I can't figure out why she got so upset," or, "Some girl I went parking with a couple of times, no big deal."

Except for Mami's snores, the house was absolutely quiet. Well, Papi could do whatever he liked. He could ground her indefinitely, make her work longer hours in the shop, or give her the beating he had spared her the night she had come home so late. And Travis could pretend those long evenings together hadn't happened at all. She felt herself beginning to match her breathing to the slow, deep rhythm of Mami's snores. And then Tom—it had been so different to kiss someone you—well, really *knew*. And liked. And cared about. And who cared about you. She wondered how they would feel when they saw each other again. Would he look sheepish and embarrassed? Would she feel shy? Oh, she wanted him to kiss her again and again. . . .

The slam of the van door made her start. Her dream had been so real. She had been dancing with Tom at the Cuban Club, only there had been crystal chandeliers instead of fluorescent ceiling panel lights, and the club combo had been transformed into a vast orchestra, conducted by a gallant old man in white tie and tails. That's right, it had been Arthur Fiedler and the Boston Pops, playing at her *quince,* just for her and Tom. . . .

She must have fallen asleep again, because when she woke up the second time the living room was dark. There was a blanket tucked around her, and she could hear Mami and Papi talking in a low murmur in the kitchen. She sat up slowly and coughed a couple of times, to clear the sleep from her throat.

"I think she's awake." She heard Mami's piercing stage whisper.

Shielding her eyes, she fumbled for the light. There! The living room looked so safe and cozy with the lamp casting soft shadows on the age-darkened wallpaper.

"Did you have a good nap?" Mami asked, coming in from the kitchen, carefully trying to hide her concern.

"Yes, but I don't even remember falling asleep. Does your stomach feel better?"

"Much better." Mami beamed. "But now it hurts from not having any food, not since last night. I'll fix us just a little supper, yes?" Luisa could smell the minute steaks sizzling in the pan. Her mouth watered and the gastric juices gurgled in her stomach.

"You must have been tired," Papi said, settling himself heavily into his reclining chair. "It's good for you to sleep. You're still growing."

Luisa steeled herself to tell Papi how sorry she was about the scene at the Blaines'. Papi was a lot more perceptive than Luisa was usually willing to give him credit for: He must have a pretty good idea now whom she had met that night at the Trumbull mall. She shot an inquiring look at him, but his head was conveniently turned to avoid meeting her eyes, although she could feel him glance at her as soon as she looked away. Papi wasn't going to mention what had happened at all, she suddenly realized.

"I haven't grown half an inch in two years," she contradicted happily.

"That's because you don't sleep enough," he persisted, and, picking up the remote control, turned on the TV. It was the last quarter of the Cowboys-Vikings game, and the stadium crowd was cheering wildly about the last play. "First down," Papi announced, "Cowboys."

Between the blaring of the radio and the full volume of the football game, Luisa didn't hear the phone ring.

"It's for you, Luisa," Mami shouted. "But we're eating dinner soon."

"If it's Mary Beth, tell her I'll call her back later."

"It's not Mary Beth," Mami said, with an odd look on her face.

Luisa took the receiver with her into the bathroom and locked the door.

"Hello?"

"Luisa, it's me, Travis. I know you told me that your parents don't like it when guys call you on the phone, but I had to talk to you."

Suddenly her knees felt a little shaky. She sat down on the edge of the toilet seat.

"Why did you run away like that this afternoon?"

If he didn't know, she wasn't going to tell him. "What do you think?"

"I think you were embarrassed to have me see you helping your dad in his reupholstery business. I don't know why you were embarrassed, but I think you were."

"I don't live in Weston, Travis."

"I know. You live at—it's written down here in my mom's address book—446 Tilden Street, Bridgeport. But what about Friday night?"

"That was Karen Cuffner's house. She goes to school with me. You met her once at the country club."

"That's right, her father works for Exxon."

"Well, my father works for Consolidated Can, when he isn't out making reupholstery deliveries. Only he works on the assembly line. Pretty glamorous, wouldn't you say?"

"Okay, I'm pretty dense," Travis said slowly. "You're probably thinking, 'What a dumb jock.' But I still don't see what the problem is. So you don't live in Weston. So your father doesn't work in an office. So you go to that wacky convent school. Why make such a big deal about it? I don't want to sound insulting, but who cares?"

"Luisa! Dinnertime!" Mami hollered.

"Coming!" she returned, and then said quietly to Travis, "I guess *I* do. Or I did. I don't know anymore. But I can't talk now—I have to go eat dinner."

"Can I call you again? I want to get this straightened out."

"Okay."

"Your parents won't mind?"

"No," Luisa admitted. "I just said that because I was afraid they'd answer the phone in Spanish if you called."

"I'll call you sometime this week then, because—Luisa,

I still want to see you if you want to see me."

The minute steaks were delicious, and Luisa had a second helping of black beans. Mami looked at her suspiciously. "Are you sure you're feeling all right?" she asked, laying her hand on Luisa's forehead. "You feel a little warm."

"I can't win," Luisa complained. "If I don't eat, Abuela wrings her hands and everyone tells me I'll be a midget. If I do eat, you want to rush me to the hospital."

"Go ahead and eat," Mami said, poising another steaming ladle of beans over Luisa's still-full plate.

"I said I would have seconds, not thirds." She felt happier than she had felt in as long as she could remember.

The doorbell rang, and Mami bustled over to answer it. She loved it when anybody dropped by at mealtime.

"Tom!" Luisa heard her exclaim. "You just in time for eat. But José no is home yet. He still out with the pizzas, I believe so."

"Thanks. I'm starving for any food that isn't pizza," Tom said. "But I didn't come to see Joey. I came to see Luisa."

CHAPTER

20

Luisa's uncle Angel leaned heavily on the horn and shouted a string of furious Spanish curses. The car ahead of him in the New York–bound lane of the Connecticut turnpike refused to move over. "I spit on your mother's grave!" he shouted. "I hope your father rots in hell!" Luisa and Mami exchanged glances and tried very hard not to laugh out loud. The shopping trip for Luisa's special dress had only been delayed—and just by a week—because the *quince* at the Cuban Club was on again.

As Luisa had predicted, the phones had been busy all week long with cousins and second cousins and second cousins twice removed comparing notes on Roberto's financial ruin. Luisa had seen Roberto and Anna once since the confrontation over Jaime's shoe box, and was both relieved and a little disappointed to find them the same as before. The two of them, with Bobby, had come over to dinner on Wednesday, and they had talked about the new movie playing at the shopping center, Roberto's upcoming trip to Brussels, Bobby's newest girl friend—everything they used to talk about, with just one exception: There was no mention of jai alai.

But if Roberto wasn't talking about jai alai anymore, everyone else was. And the good thing to come out of all the feverish gossip was that Luisa's uncle Miguel had offered to take on Roberto's debts, so Papi's money was once again available for the *quince*. Luisa thought that Roberto must mind terribly taking favors from the brother he so envied and resented. But when she mentioned it to Papi, he just snapped that Roberto wasn't in any position to complain.

143

It was going to be some party. All Luisa's Bridgeport relatives were going to be there—they hadn't all been together since her cousin Isobel's wedding, and Luisa found herself looking forward to seeing everyone again. All of Papi's friends from the factory and their families, and some of Mami and Papi's favorite reupholstery customers (not the Blaines, thank heaven) were also invited. And Mary Beth and Karen, of course, and their parents, and half a dozen other girls from Our Lady of the Mountains. Abuela had suggested that they invite some of the sisters, but Mami (dear, wonderful Mami) fortunately put her foot down there. Joey was bringing some of his friends so there'd be guys to match up with the Our Lady girls. Not that Karen and Mary Beth needed to be matched up with anyone. Karen was selecting one lucky escort from her stable of beaux, and Mary Beth, with scarcely any urging, had invited Doug. Most important, Tom would be there—he and Joey had arranged with Victor to have the night off—and Luisa could hardly wait to dance with him as she had in her dream.

The question, however, was whether Luisa should invite Travis. She closed her eyes so that Mami would think she was asleep and stop jabbering to her about party details. She had a lot of thinking to do about Travis.

He had called during the week, as he had promised, but they hadn't talked any more about whether a WASP from Trumbull and a Spic from the East Side could find happiness together. They both knew that was no longer the issue. In the end, Karen and Mary Beth and Joey and Tom had been right: The Good Times bar, the cluttered reupholstery shop, and Mami's broken English hadn't made a difference to anyone—except Luisa. She had been the one who thought it mattered so much to have a sophisticated family and an American heritage. And now—well, she guessed it didn't matter to her, either. She wouldn't trade Mami and Papi for anyone else's parents—and she wouldn't trade being Cuban, either. All along the problem had been hers—no one else's, certainly not Travis's.

To her surprise, this new information made her feel not grateful and relieved, but deeply troubled. Because if you took away the problem of Trumbull and Bridgeport, that left the problem of Travis and Luisa. She had imagined that the only thing wrong with their relationship was her private shame about her family and her background. She could never talk to him about anything that mattered to her because too much had to be kept secret. But now there were no more secrets. And she still couldn't talk to him.

Their Tuesday night telephone conversation had been just like all the others. He talked about football, while she made a polite, responsive noise every so often, glad at least that she didn't have to fix her features in apparent interest. He made some jokes about nuns, and even though she realized they weren't meant to insult her religion, she still didn't think they were funny. She laughed, anyway, just to fill the silence when he was done. But she resented having to do it. And she hardly said anything. She, who talked to Mary Beth for an hour every night, and who could talk to Tom and never notice where the hours had gone, had nothing to say to Travis.

Luisa still felt confused. She opened her left eye a little. They were just in Yonkers. That was good; it meant she had more time to try to sort this out. Okay. She loved looking at Travis and walking around with him and having people notice that she was with such a fantastic-looking guy. That was shallow of her, maybe, but it was true. She had loved falling in love, and so romantically, with a stranger from afar (meaning outside Bridgeport city limits). And the night at Karen's, when he talked to her about his father and playing baseball rather than going to college, she had really started to feel a little close to him. He had told her something about himself that wasn't easy for him to say, something that he probably hadn't told anyone else. But he hadn't opened himself up to her again—maybe he had nothing more to share—and, even after the fateful Trumbull delivery, she didn't find herself any more able to open up to him. No, now that she knew him just a little bit, she realized she wasn't in love with Travis.

She knew that because she knew now what it was to love somebody. She was in love with Tom. But it had taken thinking she was in love with Travis to make her see it.

The night of the reupholstery delivery she and Tom had gone out for a walk, as soon as he had eaten enough to keep Mami contented. Mami had looked flabbergasted when Tom suggested a walk—people in Bridgeport just didn't go for evening strolls, promenading past the bars on East Main Street. And it hadn't been a sultry summer's evening, either. The wind had been blowing off the Sound and it had been cold. But Luisa had buttoned up her hateful old jacket all the way to the top button, and once they were safely out of sight, she had slipped her mittened hand inside Tom's. Right away she had felt warmer.

They had just walked, not caring where they were going, down streets that were shabbily familiar by day but seemed strange and unfriendly after dark. Some boys had yelled something at them from a passing car, and Tom had held Luisa's hand more tightly.

They hadn't talked at all for a few blocks, and then Tom had spoken first. "Lu, what I want to know is: Was it just a dream or did I kiss you this afternoon in Victor's delivery Beetle?"

"It wasn't a dream. Or, if it was, I dreamed it, too."

"Must've been something we ate. We shouldn't eat all that heavy pizza right before we go to sleep."

Luisa had laughed. "Is it still part of the dream now, or are we awake?"

"There's only one way to tell." Then he had bent down and kissed her on the mouth, as she had tilted her face to meet his.

"Did you feel that?" he had asked. She had nodded emphatically.

"Why didn't we think of this before?" Tom had asked incredulously, after another kiss. "How could you have been such a dummkopf?"

"Me? What were you doing all this time, Mr. Know-it-all?"

"Watching you flip out over that Trumbull guy. Falling for you worse and worse. Eating my heart out."

"Oh, come on. Were you really?"

"Really. I could tell from everything Joey said, and, hell, just from looking with my own two eyes, that you thought this guy Travis was something pretty special. And I thought, How special could this guy possibly be? And the answer, the more I thought about it, was not special enough. Then I realized I didn't even need to meet Mr. Trumbull to know he wasn't right for you, and that could only be because I knew a certain someone else *was* right for you."

"Were you jealous?" Luisa had asked.

"Sure, but I'm good at waiting. I knew you couldn't go out for too long with anyone who couldn't steer your father straight about the Yankees and appreciate the way Mami sings."

"You *like* how she sings?"

"No, I don't *like* how she sings. I *love* it."

"Oh, Tom, you should have said something."

"I'm saying it now," he had said, and they had walked on, hand in hand.

Suddenly, as Angel sped across the Harlem River into Manhattan, Luisa knew exactly what she had to do about Travis. She had to tell him. Honestly. Everything. (Well, almost everything. She could leave out the little critique of his kissing style.) She wouldn't play any games or make up any stories.

If, after they had talked, he wanted to come to the *quince,* just as her friend, well, he would be more than welcome. He could even bring a date if he liked. There was one girl from Our Lady, in fact, who would be perfect for Travis. Kathleen O'Connor. She was nuts about football and could listen to stories about passes and first downs and field goals all night long. And Luisa imagined that Kathy O'Connor could choke someone with her tongue, too, if it came to that.

She felt Mami shaking her shoulder. "Luisa, baby, wake up! We're here in New York to find you the prettiest dress in the city!"

CHAPTER

21

Luisa woke up in the darkness of a December morning and realized it was her fifteenth birthday. She was a little surprised that she didn't feel any different. It wasn't that she really thought one day could make much difference. Though sometimes it did. She had certainly been changed by the day she met Travis.

But today she was fifteen! And tonight, at long last, she would have her *quince,* and she would see Tom (not that she didn't see him every single day), and he would just swoon when he saw her in the new dress. The dress was the result of a compromise with Mami. Luisa had tried on an elegant, sexy, low-cut black dress that made her look seventeen. At *least.* Mami had been tempted, too, to let her have it, but there were limits to how much Papi would be able to endure. Mami, of course, had chosen some hideous, flowered, flouncy, Spanish-looking thing. When Luisa tried it on she had looked like the flamenco dancer doll that was always tumbling off the coffee table. The compromise was a gold velvet dress with a small flowered pattern. It was simply cut and fitted Luisa beautifully.

Mami stuck her curler-festooned head in the bedroom door. Luisa quickly snapped her eyes shut and rolled over, pulling the covers tightly around her, but it was too late. "Happy birthday to you! Happy birthday to you!" Mami sang, loudly and not quite on key. Luisa covered her ears with her hands.

There were pancakes for breakfast, lots and lots of them. Luisa told Mami she wasn't very hungry, not wanting to spoil the effect of the new dress by a bulging tummy, but she ended up eating two platefuls, soaked in

149

maple syrup. She was halfway through the second, eating more and more slowly, when the doorbell rang. Mami peeked out the window and gave a delighted little shriek.

"Flowers for Miss Luisa Ruiz," the man said. Inside the long white box were fifteen yellow roses, with a card from Tom.

"Thirty dollars for flowers that won't last three days," Papi snorted, shaking his head disapprovingly, but Luisa could tell that he was pleased at her first flowers. The whole house smelled faintly of roses.

It was hard for Luisa to find a spare half hour to get ready for the party, let alone to meditate on her new adult status. Because it was a Saturday, the whole collection of *quince* celebrators paraded by. Nobody was going to have any appetite left for the Cuban Club dinner, after eating the quantity of cold cuts and Spanish pastries Mami and Abuela kept producing from the kitchen. Luisa's presents piled up all over the living room, and in between visits she furtively counted her birthday cash: $120 at three-thirty and still pouring in.

Just as she had finally slipped into the beautiful *quince* dress and brushed her hair one last time, she saw from the bedroom window a blue Mustang creeping down Tilden Street, as if looking for an unfamiliar house number. It passed the Ruizes' house and then backed up again. It had to be Travis, but what he was doing in front of her house she didn't know. She had invited him to the *quince* the evening they had had their "honest" talk, but he couldn't come. It was his parents' twentieth wedding anniversary, and they were going to New York to celebrate.

The honest talk had been an unbelievable success. There had been a party at Travis's the weekend after the *quince* shopping trip to celebrate the team's first win of he season, and Mami and Papi had said that Luisa could go if Karen was going, too. Karen *was* going, not that Karen was a very effectual chaperone. But Mami and Papi didn't have to know everything.

When Travis had first told her about the party, Luisa hadn't wanted to go. She knew he still thought of her as his girl friend, and that would be awkward—if flattering—now that she was in love with someone else. It wouldn't be easy, either, to sit primly on the edge of that pink satin sofa without remembering the occasion of its delivery: How could she have created such a humiliating spectacle, over something that mattered so little? But she couldn't postpone a heart-to-heart talk with Travis very much longer. They might as well have it at the party, she had decided.

She had been a little surprised, when she arrived at Travis's house, that it didn't seem as magnificent as she had imagined it would. His living room was just so much like Karen's, with the same velour sofa with detachable sections, the same low glass coffee table and thick, light carpet. The art on the walls even looked the same. Luisa found herself missing the happy clutter of photographs in her own living room, of the christenings, first communions, *quinces,* graduations, and weddings of half the Cubans in the western hemisphere.

Sure enough, Travis had put his arm around her in front of all his friends, and introduced her to them as his girl friend. Luisa had felt proud in a way, but she had also been more nervous about what she had to say. Travis sure hadn't made it easy.

She had waited until they were dancing to a slow song on the stereo. "Travis?"

"Mmmm?" he had murmured, kissing her hair.

"Can we go somewhere and talk?"

For answer, he had steered her into the laundry room and, without pulling the light cord over the washing machine, had begun to kiss her.

"I said *talk*."

"Shoot."

She had found the light cord in the darkness and then, once she had gotten used to the glare from the bare bulb, perched herself on the dryer so that she could look right at Travis.

"Travis, we—we don't really have very much in common," she had begun tentatively.

"What do you mean, we don't have much in common?" he had demanded, still joking around. "You're female and I'm male. That's plenty in common."

"No, really," she had said. "We don't have very much to talk about."

"Who needs to talk?"

"I need to talk. I—I can't go out with someone unless I can really talk to him about—well, everything."

"So let's talk. What do you want to talk about?"

"But, don't you see, that's just it. It doesn't come naturally to us to talk. It's something that we have to *try* to do and it shouldn't be that way."

"So what are you saying?"

He had looked hurt then, and that was what Luisa couldn't bear. She had taken a deep breath.

"I think—we shouldn't see each other any more—I mean, not like this. Oh, I like you, Travis, and I never had a crush on anyone like I've had on you—I guess that's been obvious enough—but I can't make out with someone unless we're—well, friends first."

He had stood silently for a moment and then suddenly

miled. When he did, Luisa had wondered if she was making a terrible mistake: There couldn't ever be anyone, however handsome, who could smile like that.

"I guess I feel the same way," he had said then. "I felt kind of like saying the same thing, sort of, after that night at your friend Karen's, when we watched the made-for-TV crap and knocked the pool balls around. I thought, he's cute and I could kiss her all night, but, jeez, if that's her idea of a good time, I just don't know."

"But we talked that night, remember, about baseball and your father and everything," she had said, suddenly defensive. It was one thing for her to decide she didn't want to go out with Travis. It was another for him to feel the same way about her.

"That's right," he had said. "That surprised me, my telling you all that. I usually don't confide much in people, as I guess you've noticed."

"So why didn't you say anything to me about breaking up?"

"Well, practically the next day you and your dad came over with the sofa. And then I was afraid if I suggested we cool it, you'd think it was because I looked down on your parents and where you lived or something crazy like that.

"And I just couldn't get that look on your face, before you turned and ran away, out of my mind," he had confessed. "I couldn't stand thinking that you could be so unhappy, and for nothing, really, just because of me."

"So we're friends?" she had asked, sticking out her hand.

"Friends," he had agreed, covering her hand with his.

But then they had never really gotten around to calling each other. Luisa had dialed his number once, after hearing "You'll Never Find Another Love Like Mine" on the radio at Mary Beth's, but the line had been busy and she hadn't tried again. And another day, she and Tom had passed the blue Mustang on the Merritt Parkway, going in the opposite direction, and Travis had honked and waved. Her heart had turned a somersault then, even though she wasn't in love with him anymore.

It turned another somersault now, as she heard him in the living room, talking to Papi. She emerged from the bedroom, feeling shy and self-conscious in her *quince* finery, and Travis whistled appreciatively.

"I go now warm up the truck," Papi said, and abruptly disappeared, leaving them alone.

"Happy birthday, beautiful," Travis said. "Sweet fifteen."

"But I've been kissed," she said, "thanks to you. Did you know that that night in the parking lot, outside the dance, was my first time?"

"No kidding," he said, looking as if he wanted to kiss her again, right on the spot. His eyes looked even bluer than they had the day she had met him on East Main Street.

"Travis, there's something I've been wanting to ask you."

"Shoot."

"That day we met, when you almost ran over me, where were you going? I mean, what were you doing driving down East Main Street?"

"Visiting my grandmother. She lives three or four blocks from here."

"Your grandmother lives on the East Side?"

"She certainly does. Has for the last sixty-seven years and will for the next sixty-seven, if she lives that long."

"On the East Side?"